WITHDRAWN

Quickies – 7
A Black Lace erotic short-story collection

D1638800

Look out for our themed Wicked Words and Black Lace short-story collections:

Already Published: *Sex in the Office, Sex on Holiday, Sex in Uniform, Sex in the Kitchen, Sex on the Move, Sex and Music, Sex and Shopping, Sex in Public, Sex with Strangers*

Published August 07: *Love on the Dark Side: A Collection of Paranormal Erotica from Black Lace* (short-stories and fantasies)

Quickies – 7
A Black Lace erotic short-story collection

BLACK LACE

Black Lace books contain sexual fantasies.
In real life, always practise safe sex.

This edition published in 2007 by
Black Lace
Thames Wharf Studios
Rainville Road
London W6 9HA

The Tipping Point	© Jan Bolton
Magic Fingers	© Sylvia Day
Shopping Derby	© Heather Towne
Her Brush	© Jill Bannelec
The Swimming Pool	© Caroline Martin
Customer Satisfaction	© Maya Hess

Typeset by SetSystems Limited, Saffron Walden, Essex

Printed in the UK by CPI Bookmarque, Croydon, CR0 4TD

ISBN 978 0 352 34146 4

*All characters in this publication are fictitious and any resemblance
to real persons, living or dead, is purely coincidental.*

This book is sold subject to the condition that it shall not, by way of
trade or otherwise, be lent, resold, hired out or otherwise circulated
without the publisher's prior written consent in any form of
binding or cover other than that in which it is published and
without a similar condition including this condition being imposed
on the subsequent purchaser.

The Tipping Point Jan Bolton

I must have been about six months into my
position working as a research assistant for Lord X
when he let it be known that he had an enthusiasm for 'uncustomary caprices'. Given that this
information was imparted with a large leathery
hand on my bottom, there could be little doubt that
he was referring to whims of a sexual nature. But
quite how 'uncustomary' Lord X's fancies would
turn out to be was something of a shock, even to a
young woman with a fair degree of intimate
experience under her belt. I'd heard that the upper
echelons of older-generation male politicians were
prone to enjoying curious pastimes now and then,
and, when such proclivities made their way into
the tabloids, I must confess that I always tittered
at the salacious details. Despite my prurient
interest in scandal in high places, I never expected
to be a party to kinky behaviour at first hand,
although, looking back, I guess I almost willed my
involvement in it to happen.

I've always found secret societies and covert
clubs so thrilling. As a child I delighted in making
up passwords and creating mock official docu-
ments out of old bills and photo-booth pictures,
swearing my friends to secrecy and hiding packets
of cigarettes in old hardback books that I'd cut the

guts from. The hidden and the encoded; the clandestine and the curious − these are the things to which I am drawn.

I also like prising secrets out of people about their sex lives. During tipsy conversations at university girls' nights in, I'd always steer the topic to erotic matters, trying to coerce my colleagues into saucy confessions. They never admitted to anything particularly memorable: a bit of light bondage, a few sex toys, some dressing up. Of course, no one in my circle of bright young things would go into details more scandalous than elliptical chat about silk scarves and ice cubes; the sort of thing women's magazines recommend to spice up your love life. None of them spoke about the emotions and thoughts they'd had while intimately engaged with their Jessica Rabbit, or fastened to a bed post with handcuffs. It was all very 'what I did in my bedroom' − the almost-to-be-expected behaviour of young lovers. I'll bet that few of them had indulged in what I found myself doing over the course of that dull damp winter of 1999.

It is fair to mention at this point that my behaviour during the weeks leading up to Lord X's announcement had been somewhat flirtatious. I was trying to wheedle myself into his good books for a recommendation that would better my chances of an increase in salary. I'd heard that a number of senior research positions were due to become available, some with postings abroad, and, if I could secure a place on one of them, I would be looking at having a very handsome CV by the time I was 25 and possibly a civil service post that would set me up for many career years to come. So my reaction was not entirely one of surprise when he rose to my teasing bait, and it took considerable effort not to betray how pleased I was with myself for having had this effect on him so easily. Of course, one must never reveal a trace of triumph to Alpha types like Lord X that you have manipulated them, or that you can read them like an open book – for that would ruin their own sense of achievement in the sport, and sport is, after all, a pastime in which Alpha types love to excel. So I engineered my expression into one of feminine fluster on that cloudy Wednesday in November and waited for him to elaborate. Before I tell you what that was, I think I'd better recap, to describe exactly what was happening to prompt such an unprofessional detour from political matters in hand.

For months I had been assisting Lord X in the preparation of a counterpoint paper concerning the extension of bus lanes and road tolls to peripheral areas of London. The whole business was becoming so deathly dull that I began to wish I had opted for my second career choice in the Royal Navy. Yet here I was in the chambers of Parliament itself, with my foot on the first rung of a career in politics. I couldn't give up because of some tiresome rigmarole for the Transport Committee. I was, for the most part, delighted to be there; there were fewer buildings in the world more esteemed than the Houses of Parliament.

I'll always remember, setting foot into the Lords' chamber for the first time, how the weight of English history and tradition, with all its trappings

of pomp and privilege, and ermine-cloaked authority, had struck me in the gut as something of a
pleasant surprise. I had feared I would find the
sombre ceremonies moribund and irrelevant in a
London that pulsed to a sound more evocative of
South Central Los Angeles than Westminster, but,
in fact, the reverse was true. Witnessing a debate
on my first day in the House, I felt a sense of pride
– to be British and to be part of a majestic contin-
uum. Here was something not dowdy, but mighty;
for goodness sake, I walked past a document no
less profound than the Magna Carta on my way to
the canteen every day.

Every part of the building was steeped in tradition. Not for me a staff room of table football and
plasma screens tuned to MTV. The décor of the
office in which we worked could not have changed
much from the 1940s. With heavy wooden-panel-
ling on the walls, solid oak desks, thick Turkish
carpet and book shelves lining one complete side
of this vast room, it had an air of constitutional
propriety about it. One couldn't imagine anything
more frivolous occurring in this environment than
perhaps taking a nip from the odd bottle of single
malt that was locked in one of the desk drawers.
And yet, paradoxically, it was this stifling ambi-
ance, I'm sure, that was conducive to the extremi-
ties that Lord X – and those like him – went in
finding pleasure through very private means out of
Parliament hours.

It was about 4.30 in the afternoon; almost dark
outside with the central heating turned up far too

high for my liking – a time when drowsiness can set in and the listlessness that questions the point of analysing yet another focus-group report.

I became aware that Lord X had been watching me at particular points during my trips up and down the bookshelves, ascending and descending the step-ladder to retrieve any number of lever-arch files dedicated to 1997's research findings.

It was my ascents that seemed to catch his eye the most, however; I spotted him looking at me through discreet glances over my shoulder. It was true that I'd begun to wear increasingly flattering outfits to work. Of course I wasn't sporting anything too dressy or showy, and certainly not revealing, but I selected garments that showed my firm rounded figure to its best advantage: plunging V-shaped necklines, wide-hemmed, tailored trousers and, on this occasion, a crisp cotton white shirt and a satin-lined, very formal-looking navy-blue skirt with a vent cut into the back and a column of 2″ wide buckles that formed a vertical line from the waistband to the base of my spine.

I made my way backwards and forwards, selecting files and photocopying them before carefully replacing them and scaling the ladder, which was fixed into the floor on smooth runners, to put them back in order.

It transpired that the vision of my bottom, flaring under my waistline into two perfect globes, clad tightly in my business skirt, reached what Cartier-Bresson coined the 'decisive moment' at about 4.33p.m., just after the huge clang of Big Ben, when the silence of the room was broken by Lord X's rejoinder, 'I love it when your skirt raises just a little. It does brighten up a dull afternoon.'

He then immediately coughed and croaked – a nervous reaction to the suddenness of his inappropriate outburst, as if it had issued forth of its own volition and he was fighting to prevent further unconscious desires bursting through. He sounded as if his arousal was choking him and had to be outed lest he would strangle.

I froze on the ladder, considering the magnitude of repercussions that could ensue as a result of such a proclamation. For a few torturous seconds he must have anticipated a torrent of feminist fury, a raft of disciplinary procedures and claims of sexual harassment appearing on House of Commons internal memos ... the unspeakable procedure that these days is so likely to spiral out from an older gentleman's more sporting observations.

Any fears he may have had were dispatched as swiftly to the wastebin as an email request for charity sponsorship as I turned 45 degrees to the left and regarded him from my lofty position. Despite his being so much older, at least 50, and being my employer, I just couldn't resist a tease. I patently avoided referring to his announcement and asked him instead, 'Would you want me to look in the older files, sir, like those positioned on the top shelf just a row along from your desk? I would have to reach up even higher to get at them.'

'Oh, yes,' he stammered. 'Yes, that's a very good idea.'

I slowly descended the ladder, swaying my hips and presumably whetting his appetite even more. I pushed the ladder along, looking him in the eye as he settled in for the display. When I got to the perfect point in the tracks I once again ascended the metal steps. The old goat was now shamelessly craning his neck, looking right up my skirt as I bent one knee to lean onto the flat level top of the ladder. In this position he was getting a shadowy view of my crotch and the swollen pouch of my sex pressed tight and plump against the cotton of my knickers, just visible to him as a flash of white.

His eyes darted about, shining as he became playful, to settle on some long-filed tome. 'Townsend, I need you to reach for Policy and Practice in Highway Reform,' he said.

This old, brown-leather book was just possible to reach from where I had placed the ladder but it would require a stretch long enough to send my skirt riding up to at least the bottom of my knickers. Still, there was little point being genuinely coy at this stage, and I swallowed my pride and went for it, wriggling slightly as the skirt lifted to show the tops of my hold-ups and two slivers of flesh at the base of my meaty bottom.

He let out a groan of appreciation.

Before I treated him to too much excitement, I kneeled up straight, pulled my skirt back down as if nothing had happened and began flicking through the onion-skin pages, resting the base of the heavy book on my pubic bone as I looked for mind-numbing facts and figures that I could recite about transport reform, prolonging the sweet agony, imagining what lusty desires were coursing through his imagination, and how hard he would be in his trousers.

'Did you know, sir,' I began, 'that they drove sheep through Chalk Farm until war broke out in 1939?' I feigned an engrossed interest in the weighty file. 'And tram lines ran all the way to Primrose Hill, right up until 1952.'

'Well, I think I had better see that for myself,' said Lord X, obviously suffering exquisite torment at my stringing out this curious seduction. He surely could not have expected a reaction more animated at best than a flush of girly giggles, and now I was showing him my knickers and teasing him mercilessly.

'Bring it to me without delay,' he boomed.

I knew he was excited beyond measure that I hadn't scolded him for taking our working relationship into this potentially dangerous new zone of mixing pleasure with business. A sense of relief and of pure devilment must have been running around his veins, his pulse racing with lewd anticipation at the thought of getting his hands on me. I dragged it out even more.

'Lord X,' I began, beginning to introduce a girly inflection to my intonation, 'if I bring it right over to you and lay it on your desk, would we be able to look at it together?

'Of course, my dear,' he said, his voice tight with lust. 'But, before you do, I think I'd like to test the safety levels of that ladder, what with you balancing those heavy files. I wouldn't want you to fall or have an accident due to my negligence.'

He pushed his chair away from the desk – enough to show that my assumptions were spot on; his crotch was straining with tension due to an almighty tumescence. He adjusted himself and walked over to where the ladder was positioned and stood beneath it. I knew what was coming – and what he wanted. Call it sexual intuition, but I knew he didn't want me to descend just yet. I placed the book on the top platform and slowly began to lift my skirt once more. I could feel the tension in my calves; my heart beating in reaction to my daring display, and a slick warmth beginning to pool between my legs. My sex lips were swollen and moist; it felt as if they were blooming to full shape – into the ripe pouch that looks so inviting to men and yet is, for the most part, a sight not experienced by the female – unless she has a habit of studying herself in the mirror from behind.

Lord X was about three or four feet beneath me. Somehow the distance added to the spectacle, as he kept telling me to stay where I was so he could 'admire the view from on high'. I leaned forwards once more and this time added to the display by sliding my right hand between my legs and rubbing the tight cotton that covered the pouch.

'You dirty girl,' said Lord X. 'Playing with yourself in my office. It's a disgrace. I think you should show me exactly what you would do left to your own devices.'

'Well, that would mean I would have to take my knickers down,' I said, affecting a voice not entirely commensurate with one who has an MSc in Political Sciences.

'Oh no you don't,' said Lord X. 'I'll be the judge of that.'

And then the ladder wobbled slightly as he stepped up two levels, within touching distance of my arse.

'Feel how tight they are, sir,' I complained. 'I can't possibly do what I want to do with knickers this tight around me.'

'I suppose you want to play with yourself, eh? Want to make yourself orgasm in my office.'

I nodded my head. And then it came – a firm and gentle caress of my bottom cheeks with the heel of his hand and slowly, slowly, a thick curled finger slipped under the gusset and into my hot juicy centre.

'Oh, Townsend,' he croaked, 'I think we've got a situation here.'

He levered his arm to a position that gave him maximum potential for manipulation, and began to go at fingering me with the enthusiasm of a teenaged boy getting his first feel of a girl, but tempered with the experience of remembering to rub over my button with each alternate stroke

'Do you like that?' he whispered into my ear. 'Do you like me touching your dirty little cunt like this?'

'I think it's disgusting, sir,' I replied. 'You should know better, a man of your position. What will the Transport Committee say when you tell them your report was postponed because you had to rub your young assistant between the legs and make her climax.'

'I'll tell them it was your fault, you little minx,' he said, entering into my fantasy of inappropriate honesty. 'I'll tell them I had a hard-on so big that neither of us could concentrate on Highway Reform Policy. And, speaking of which, Townsend, you're going to make me do something I might regret if you don't get down off the ladder now. I'm about to shoot in my pants when I'd rather be doing it all over your sweet little face with my hands on your arse.'

He was now shamelessly masturbating. He'd freed himself from his trousers while he'd been fingering me, and I could now snatch glimpses of his penis shining like a rude beacon in the almost hallowed room. I was imagining what it would feel like to descend the ladder and sit right on it, or take it into my mouth and suck on it as I squatted under his desk. More pertinently, I wondered what it would be like to have it thrust into me from behind. It was, I suppose, what one would call the tipping point.

I descended the ladder with his hands on my backside and the air thick with tension and the scent of our combined arousal. I then hurried to lock the door so that we wouldn't be interrupted. In the meantime, he tucked himself away for a moment while he reached into his drawer and produced two glasses and a bottle of vintage red wine. His restraint impressed me; I was so hot and moist in my sex that it was literally aching for attention, yet he seemed calm and able to control his lusts, despite what he had said.

'Look, you won't think badly of me if we have a little recreation time, will you, Townsend?' he began, suddenly businesslike and observing me over the top of his varifocals.

'I wouldn't be here now if that were likely,' I said, still the coquette. 'I don't want to cause any trouble ... I just, well, I think you would probably appreciate me more than men my own age, and I would like to give you an afternoon to remember.'

I meant the flattery, too. I was bored with vain go-getters that were my contemporaries; the City boys and snooty girls who bullied their way up the career ladder without a trace of humility. For all his power and standing in society, Lord X had old-fashioned Class with a capital C and an education that had taught him manners and good grace, even in the most compromising of moments – such as adjusting one's genitals in female company.

I touched his arm very lightly with one finger, looked into his eyes with a cheeky expression and bit my bottom lip. It was then that the brown leathery hand made its way to my bottom, and he leaned in closer to me so that I could smell his lemony cologne and a whiff of quality leather. Despite the fact we were alone, and no one could hear, he whispered into my ear – a gesture so discreet and understated that a thrill of illicit pleasure ran through me like a dart of sexual energy. It was then that I was informed of the 'uncustomary caprices'.

I giggled softly into my hand and wriggled myself against him.

'I do like a game girl,' he said. 'I like to be able to see things and say things.'

I could feel his erection poking into the top of my hip as I took my first sip of the fruity red wine and kept looking straight ahead. I wondered what it was he liked to see and say but I made a bet with myself at very short odds that it would involve my bottom and his verbal appreciation of it.

I began to question him about what exactly it was he liked to see and say as we clinked glasses and settled into stringing out our arousal until it reached bursting point.

'How about two girls together, rubbing each other between the legs?' I ventured.

'Well, that would be pretty, but they would have to be absolutely filthy with each other, and very natural ... not like those silicone monstrosities from California.'

'Is it to watch a live sex show or lap-dancer?'

'Christ, no!' he thundered, then laughed. 'Watch some bored tart fold her drug-ravaged body around a greasy pole ... no thanks.'

They're not all like that,' I countered, realising swiftly that I had neither met nor ever spoken to such a person. 'What about those "gentlemen's clubs"?' I offered.

'They're all right, I suppose, but it's all too Americanised for my liking. Too much toothpaste and hairspray. None of them has that, that ...'

'Understated Englishness?' I ventured.

'Exactly!' he said, as if I had hit on something quintessential. 'I don't want some brassy scrubber writhing around all over the place. I don't see the point. Some of them are quite pretty, I suppose, but they all seem too experienced. None of them has the right air of naughtiness about them. No, I want a dirty English girl with a good education and an adventurous spirit.'

He sat back on his chair and patted his knees, so I sat down sideways on top of him. He snuck a hand round me and into my shirt, and then whispered in my ear in a mock-admonishing voice, 'Oh Townsend, I'm disappointed that you didn't know what I wanted.'

I swivelled my head towards him, getting the chance to study him at close range. His hair was thick, grey and wavy. His eyes were clear blue and his skin well cared for.

'You were supposed to go over my knees, not down on top of them,' he exclaimed.

The thought hadn't occurred to me, and I chided myself for not being more intuitive to his predilections.

'Does that mean, that ... that...' I began fearfully.

'Oh yes. It means exactly what you are thinking, my girl. You are going to get some old-fashioned discipline meted out on your sweet, darling little bottom. But don't think I will spare you just because you are pretty,' he said. 'In fact, it'll be extra hard because of it!'

With one fluid movement he stood up, making

me slide off his lap to my feet. Before I had the chance to decide for myself whether or not this was a good idea, he flipped me onto his lap and had pulled me over his thighs. I suddenly found myself in an ignominious position, blood rushing to my head, staring at the carpet.

And then came the moments he relished. The large leathery hand caressed flat circles over my cheeks. The curling meaty finger snaked into my crevice. The practised touch of decades of pleasing wives and mistresses played under my knickers and over my clit. It was the ecstasy before the punishment.

After such tender ministrations he pulled my white cotton knickers down over my globes and laid me bare. Then came the action. The flat palm came whacking down onto my flesh in ten rapid smarting strokes.

'You dirty girl. You've been asking for it for so long. Since your first day, in fact,' he growled.

I yelped in indignation.

'What! Why?' I sobbed, as the next ten whacks landed onto my increasingly hot arse.

I wriggled and struggled, trying to free myself from his enthusiastic spanking.

'You have been trying to distract me since the very day I interviewed you,' he said, now pinching my reddened cheeks. 'Don't think you can get one over on me; I full well know the wiles of females.'

How could he have known? I had not given anything away. His pinching was an insult to my injured bottom and I began to wriggle fervently as his left hand pressed down more firmly on my back.

To temper his cruelty, an occasional tender caress was applied, and I realised that I had fallen into the hands of a master spanker and expert in female strategy. Despite the smarting sensation in my bottom, my sex was wetter than ever, and what I needed and craved was for him to give me the pounding I so rightly deserved. I could feel his hard prick pressing into me through his trousers and after another ten strokes of his hand he released me to fall like a rag doll onto the carpet. It felt natural to effect a sulky expression to add to my naughty girl persona and, when I looked up at him through tear-stained eyes, I looked right into the fleshy column that protruded from between his legs and was being pumped by his right hand.

'I've got something girls like you can't wait to get inside them,' he teased, luring me to wrap my mouth around it. 'I bet you want this, don't you?'

I crawled up his legs and laid my head in his lap. He stroked my hair tenderly, yet this was accompanied by a very stern announcement.

'I'm going to do it all over your face in a second. And I want you to love it. You're going to get my spunk in your mouth and love it.'

'But, Lord X,' I protested. 'You just said I was going to get it inside me. Properly, I mean.'

'Oh you will,' he promised, 'but all in good time.'

And with that he cupped one hand around the back of my head and brought me into close quarter with the right honourable member. It was a clean and musky column of handsome gristle and I set about it with relish. He liked to manipulate it, and took delight in rubbing it across my face, prodding it into my neck and nose and making sure I was fully acquainted with it before ordering me to open wide and take it fully into my mouth. He groaned, gasped and laughed a satisfied chuckle of a man who had got himself an unexpected treat.

I licked and sucked and pressed a hand against his balls, still snug in their pinstripe home. I was, by now, creaming into my swollen sex and completely desperate to come. I knew there would be no chance of his seeing to my needs once he'd had his fun, so I had to take matters into my own hand. With one hand skilfully playing with his cock as I took it into my mouth, I reached down and felt the pool of oozing warmth between my thighs. I pressed two fingers against my clit, not moving my hand frantically but allowing my hips to do the work, thrusting back and forth across my hand as if I were a man fucking a woman.

The sight of my abandoned display was all it took for Lord X to reach his ultimate moment. He pulled out of my mouth and told me to look up at him. The very next second he shouted out my name, shot a jet of milky fluid onto my face; then another and yet more, until my face and neck were liberally splattered.

I couldn't hold back. The combination of the sound spanking and my own teasing of him had conspired to make me more turned on than I had ever been in my life. It was the first time I'd been spanked, and the firm mastery he had inflicted on my bottom had brought out the bad girl in me – which, in turn, brought out the pretend stern taskmaster in him. It was a perfect match. It gave me an illicit thrill of confidence, and I knew the sight of me enjoying my own orgasm would be something he'd want more of.

'Watch me, sir,' I cooed. 'I'm going to come for you. You've made me have such dirty thoughts about you.'

And with that I let go – and felt myself spasm into the delicious abyss, as Lord X stroked my hair with a tender touch.

We relaxed with the wine for a while, stunned into silence at first but soon exchanging glances that glittered with the promise of future erotic fun.

It wasn't long before I was accepting lifts home, and days out to country pubs and walks in the woods under the guise of research into rural transport initiatives. The more outrageous and exhibitionist my behaviour became, the more I found myself being treated to wonderful lunches and special favours. Increasingly I allowed him to indulge his ever-more outrageous kinks.

I bared my bottom over a farmer's gate and was treated to a hearty hand-spanking with the threat of dog-walkers surprising us at any minute. He didn't care who caught us, and I admired his gusto. Once, while caught short in the New Forest after we'd polished off two bottles of wine, he begged me to let him watch as I relieved myself – except he wouldn't let me take my knickers off. He made me pee onto the ground through my knickers, which he loved. He masturbated over me as I humiliated myself before him. It was so very, very wrong, and it felt so very, very good, and my drunken laughter rang out in the autumn air as I wet myself for his amusement. And he thrashed me afterwards, too – but not very hard – with a handful of birch twigs as we made a pact to be as naughty as possible, as often as possible. I remember being driven home that day, knickerless and glowing with the delicious thrill of having behaved so impeccably filthily for my Lord.

There are so many naughty things we did, Lord X and I. We were a perfect complement to each other, despite the gap in ages between us. Those winter nights that led up to the new millennium whizzed by in a blur of tempered ribaldry. I accompanied him to soirées on the Parliament terrace, brandishing files and policy reports and being every inch the serious-minded assistant, while, barely an hour beforehand, I would have been on all fours in a Knightsbridge dungeon.

These days I head up my own research team. In summer 2000 I got my foreign posting, out to Belize where giant lizards bake in the afternoon sun and a trip to the coral reefs costs a fraction of a weekend in a New Forest hotel.

Lord X and I occasionally bump into each other at London gatherings. Why, only last month we were at a directors' convention in Pall Mall. I was entertaining some clients in a rather grand reception room lined with books. I heard a familiar voice behind me, addressing one of the young, attractive silver service staff in the most beguiling tone: 'Oh look, there's the book on social policy that I edited back in 1976. Would you mind reaching up there, my dear, seeing as you are so much younger than I?'

He watched in subtle appreciation as she scaled the ladder fixed in runners and stretched to reach the book as she teetered on the platform.

I smelt a tang of lemony cologne, and a whiff of leather as a whisper came in my ear. 'Happy days, Townsend. Happy days.'

Magic Fingers Sylvia Day

'Does that feel good?' he purred in a voice soaked in sexual intent.

Alison buried her face in the mattress and groaned. Strong, masculine fingers kneaded the length of her spine with blatant skill until the pleasure was almost too much, her body vibrating with sensations that radiated outward from his touch and pooled in her core.

She fought off the overwhelming urge to give in to an orgasm while, against her will, her back arched into his palms.

'You're so responsive,' he murmured. 'The slightest movement of my hands and your body replies.'

Her insides melted at the approval in his tone. She wanted to roll over, to have those hands caress her breasts, pinch her nipples. Lord, how she loved to have her breasts played with and they were heavy now, swollen in anticipation of his attention. Her nipples strained, peaked hard and waiting for the clasp of his fingertips.

'A little harder?' he queried, his deep, rumbling voice promising untold carnal delights. 'A little faster? A little deeper?' His wicked mouth dropped lower. 'Tell me what you need, Alison ... what you want, so I can give it to you.'

She shivered. She wanted to tell him to dip those magic fingers between her legs, rub her, stroke inside her, make her come.

But she couldn't say those things.

Her body didn't care though, and her legs parted anyway, in silent invitation.

His hands slid down and cupped her bare buttocks, kneading them. She groaned. He was killing her. She would die if he didn't take her. Right now.

His lips brushed her ear. 'Time's up,' he whispered.

Her hands clenched into fists and she wanted to cry. Five days of torture. She had to be a masochist.

Alison sat up, not bothering to hold the towel to her full breasts. What did it matter? She wouldn't be seeing him again.

His breath caught in his throat.

She looked up quickly and for an instant she imagined lust hidden in the azure blue of his intense gaze. And then there was nothing but a professional, impersonal smile as he handed her the thick terrycloth robe with the resort's logo embroidered on the front.

She shook her head ruefully as she slid off the massage table and covered herself. Wishful thinking. It went hand in hand with the torrid fantasies she'd been having at night.

'Thank you, James.' She managed a smile, even though her entire body ached with unfulfilled desire. 'It's been a pleasure.' She moved towards the door.

'See you tomorrow, Alison.'

She turned and tried to make her mouth curve

again, but couldn't. She drank him in one last time, thirsting for him. He was tall, dark, built like a warrior and with the gentle hands of an angel. Dark, thick brown hair fell over a strong brow, framing beautiful eyes the colour of the ocean just outside the door. He was gorgeous, every inch of him, from the austerely masculine beauty of his face to the sculpted body built for pleasure.

'I won't be seeing you again,' she informed him. 'I'm checking out tomorrow.'

He arched a brow, clearly surprised. 'Oh. I didn't know.' He paused, as if he were waiting for something. The moment stretched out, becoming uncomfortable.

She wanted to touch him, just once, just to see what he felt like, just for the thrill of it. She wanted to bury her face in his throat and smell the scent of his skin. She wanted to lick him, all over.

She wanted. Badly.

'Goodbye,' she choked out miserably as she fled the room.

Alison sat at her lonely table at the outdoor buffet and pushed grilled tilapia and fresh pineapple around her plate with a fork. The meal was delicious, but she couldn't eat. Her gaze lifted and moved leisurely over the multitude of diners, the tempting aroma of delicacies from every continent and some favorite local dishes drifting over her in the tropical breeze.

It was dusk, the deep orange of the sun sinking into the clear blue of the Jamaican water. She looked off the patio to the private beach below. It was empty now, but during the day it was packed with travellers, some of whom she'd convinced to come here.

In appreciation for the amount of traffic her travel agency brought to the resort, the general manager regularly sent her free vouchers. Usually she gave them away during promotions she ran to advertise her business. This year, feeling restless, she'd decided to come to the resort herself, to live a little.

'Isn't James divine?' cooed a throaty feminine voice just beyond her right shoulder. 'I could eat him alive.'

'Definitely,' agreed the voice's companion. 'The best thing about this resort is that yummy masseur. I'd have five appointments a day if they'd let me.'

The throaty voice dropped conspiratorially. 'I slipped him my spare room key today.'

'Carla!' her friend exclaimed in astonishment. 'You didn't!'

'I did,' Carla replied smugly. 'He seemed especially hot for it today. And I'm hot to give it to him.'

Alison sighed miserably and pushed her plate away. She'd first heard about James from a similar conversation a week ago. Then she'd heard the same story replayed over and over again. Breakfast, lunch and dinner, female guests at the resort raved about the to-die-for masseur with the sinful voice and blessed hands. After two days, she'd made an appointment for a massage. And after two minutes with James she'd been drowning in lust. He certainly had a rare gift.

Like an addict, she'd returned to the small hut every day of her holiday for another hour of his sweet torment. She'd kept hoping her desire would ease, but instead it had only grown worse until now she was permanently turned on, her body achingly prepped for sex. Even her vibrator could not ease her need for James, hot and hard, thrusting into her.

She was leaving the next morning and she'd never see him again. She was already experiencing the withdrawal symptoms.

Alison rose from her chair and headed towards the bar.

In her fantasies, she believed she was the only one James talked to in a sexually suggestive manner. She imagined that he was hot for her and her alone. That he waited as eagerly for their appointments as she did, and that he relished the opportunity to touch her bare skin and knead away her troubles.

In reality, she discerned from eavesdropping that James talked to all the female guests as if they were his next sexual conquest. She was nothing special; he treated her no different.

Leaning against the bar, she ordered a Red Stripe with a shot of Appleton. Downing the shot, she took the beer and strolled out to the beach to watch the sun set. Even at night the air was warm, the breeze a light caress. Alison closed her eyes and took a deep breath.

She wasn't the type of woman who had one-night stands, but she'd have one with James. She wondered if it was loneliness that made her so susceptible to indulging in her fantasy of sex with a stranger. She'd spent a week in a foreign country, alone. A quiet person by nature, she wasn't good at making friends and so had hardly spoken a word to anyone in the last seven days. She'd thought it would be relaxing after the never-ending phone calls she dealt with at work.

It wasn't relaxing. It was boring. And lonely.

Finishing her beer, Alison turned and walked back to the hotel. She slid her keycard into the lock and stepped into her room. Being on the second floor, she'd felt safe keeping the windows open. She wrinkled her nose when she saw that the maid had closed the sliding glass door and drawn the blackout curtains. When the door shut behind her, she was plunged into darkness. She moved towards the bed and the light next to it.

'Would I be wrong in thinking you want me to fuck you?'

She stilled in shock as the deeply sexual voice curled around her in the obsidian room. She went from tingling arousal to raging desire in the space of one shuddering breath.

'James?' she whispered. She sensed movement in the darkness, but heard nothing.

'Would I be wrong, Alison?' he asked again.

She swallowed hard, her hands clenching into fists. 'No.'

He sighed. Then she heard movements, sounds of him disrobing, baring his luscious body. She could scarcely breathe. With shaking hands, she reached for the lamp.

'Don't,' he murmured as if he could see her.

'Why?'

'You'll feel me better if your sense of sight is diminished.'

Her hand fluttered to her throat. *Feel him.* 'I want to admire your body.'

'Next time,' he promised in a rumbling caress of sound.

She sank on to the edge of the bed, her buckling knees no longer supporting her. *Next time.*

He'd take all night making love to her, she knew. He was just that kind of man, potently virile. She heard the tear of a foil packet and the sound of latex stretching. She could barely think, her imagination running away from her.

He came to her unerringly in the darkness, sinking to his knees before her. Laying his head in her lap, his breath left his lungs in a rush as her palms settled on his shoulders. She flexed her fingers, feeling his taut muscles and warm skin. With her fingertips she urged his chin upward. Then she bent forward to bury her face in the curve of his neck as she'd longed to do for days.

'Alison.' Her name floated through the room on a pained whisper. 'Damn you.'

She stilled, her tongue pressed against the salty column of his throat, unsure of what she had done to anger him. At her hesitation, he pulled her to the floor.

With his heated hands on her thighs and endless patience, he pushed her short sundress upward with painful slowness, kneading the skin he exposed.

'What have I done?' she asked breathlessly, her hands fisting into the carpet as he stoked her arousal.

His mouth dropped to her thigh and pressed a hot, open-mouthed kiss there. Her eyes slid closed as she gave up the effort to see him. He lifted her leg and tongued the hollow behind her knee. She shivered.

'You were going to leave,' he growled, his hot breath gusting across the sensitive skin of her inner thigh. 'After five days of torturing me with your body, allowing me to touch you without truly touching you, you were going to leave without having my cock in you.'

Her eyes flew open and she arched upward into his mouth, unbearably aroused by his blunt speech. 'James.'

'I couldn't ask you,' he said in a groan, his mouth moving upward. 'If I was wrong about the signals you were sending, if you complained, I'd be in deep shit.'

Her hands came up and her fingers shifted through his silky hair, massaging his scalp. 'You asked,' she pointed out.

'Because you didn't. And time was running out.' He spread her thighs and tongued her through her damp thong. From deep in his throat came gratifying sounds of pleasure. 'God, I knew you'd be ready for me.' He nuzzled her with his face. With a harsh tug, he tore the skimpy piece of lace away and buried his mouth in her wetness.

Her orgasm wasn't far off. Five days of foreplay and fantasy and repeated sessions with her vibrator had kept her on the edge of a powerful climax. As his tongue entered her with obvious skill, her body tensed expectantly. It was too much – the combination of the anticipation, his pursuit and the culmination of her fantasies all at once.

'I don't do these things,' she gasped. 'I don't have sex with people I don't know.'

In response, his mouth surrounded her clitoris and sucked. Hard.

Her climax hit her with full force, tearing through her body, shuddering against his mouth, pouring over his tongue.

She was still spasming when he rose and knelt before her, drawing her legs across his thighs. With his hands on her hips, he lifted her up and pulled her slowly on to his erection. Oversensitised from the power of her orgasm, her body resisted his entry, but he pressed forward inexorably.

To her surprise and delight, he was built beautifully all over. In her fantasies, she'd made him superiorly well endowed. In reality, he was. All of her life, her sex partners had been average in size. James was anything but. She writhed on the floor as he filled her, taking his time, making her feel every inch.

'Does that feel good?' he asked when she moaned long and loud. He flexed his hips and sunk in further.

'You know it does,' she whispered hoarsely.

'Did you dream of this, Alison?' He pumped in

and out twice, drugging thrusts that stroked all the right places. 'I did.'

Alison was startled by the admission. Was he telling the truth? Did he do these things, say these things, to other guests?

As he began a slow, steady, expert fucking, she found she didn't care. Not right now. He could have been with the willing Carla. Instead, he'd taken a risk on her.

He paused, keeping her impaled while his strong, well-worked hands slid under her dress, down her torso, and cupped her breasts.

'Yesss,' she hissed with pleasure.

James chuckled. 'Tell me what you need, Alison,' he coaxed. 'Tell me how to please you, tell me what you like.'

His magic fingers plucked at the aching points, twisting them, tugging them. 'I can feel the pulling of your nipples on my cock,' he whispered, flexing inside her in response. 'I knew it would be like this, you're so responsive.'

She arched into his palms, into his penis. 'Only for you.'

He groaned and, holding her tits in his hands, he resumed his thrusting. And deep inside, the heat curled. Hot and heavy, spreading outward until she was inundated with sensation.

James's heavy breathing thrilled her, his convulsive grip on her breasts excited her, his appreciative murmurs pleasured her, and through it all, her fantasies satisfied her. Her pussy clenched – once, twice. She tried to hold it off, tried to make it last.

'Don't,' he grunted, tweaking her nipples. 'I've

already waited long enough.' One of his hands reached between their legs, his thumb pressing against where they joined, feeling himself sliding into her. His fingers rested over her clit, rubbing against it with every downward stroke. With a low moan, she came, convulsing around his invading hardness until he joined her, flooding her with burning heat.

'Come on, Alison,' he murmured, as he tucked her closer into his side. 'Let's go for a walk.'

She whimpered, half asleep and afraid to move. Afraid to find out it was all a dream. 'Don't want to,' she grumbled.

'I hope you don't think I'm done. After five days of teasing, I'm just getting started.'

Her head turned towards his, trying vainly to see him, and his firm lips connected with hers. A kiss.

He kissed like he made love, with expert awareness and casual skill. With a tilt of his head, he altered the angle, granting him deeper access for the velvet stroking of his tongue. Alison moaned into his mouth, instantly awake and vibrantly aroused.

Everything was so new to her. She didn't do things like this; she didn't attract men who looked like James.

She pulled back slightly. 'Is there anything you don't do well?' she asked and felt his smile curve against her mouth.

He stood and pulled her up with him. Reaching down, he gathered up her dress and pulled it over her head. 'Did you think about me fucking you, Alison, when I massaged your body?'

'Yes,' she admitted. 'All the time.'

He reached for his shorts and she felt the heavy weight of his erection brush against her leg. When he stood, she wrapped her hands around it.

'How did I take you?' he asked in a choked voice as she stroked him softly, gently.

'Every way.'

He groaned as she tightened her grip.

'But I could always see you.'

His hand at her wrist stilled her movements. 'When we get outside you can see as much of me as you want.'

Her hands brushed along his ribs, admiring his lean strength as he dressed. 'Hurry.'

James straightened and bent forward, his wicked tongue swirling around the shell of her ear before dipping inside. She shivered with longing, ready to feel him inside her again. But he laced his fingers with hers and tugged her towards the door.

They moved with haste through the hotel, staying in the shadows when possible until they reached the private beach.

In the darkness the water was black, rippling with moonlight and soothing as it lapped rhythmically against the shore. All along the coast, the twinkling lights of various resorts competed with the brilliant stars above. It was beautiful, simply breathtaking, and a sight she would have missed if James hadn't come for her.

A fence bisected the beach, separating the resort from the public area beyond. James led her into the warm water, taking her around the barrier. He pulled her away from the place where he was an employee and she was a guest to an area where they were no more than lovers enjoying the magic of the Caribbean.

He turned to her, all moonlit beauty, a Roman statue's physical perfection come to life.

'Why me?' she couldn't help asking.

He shrugged and drew her closer, into his arms. He threw the question back at her. 'Why me?'

Before she could answer, he reached for her breast, palming it, squeezing it, robbing her of thought.

'Alison. Tell me about your fantasies. Everything.'

The gentle waves surged softly around them as she flushed in embarrassment. She wasn't like him. She didn't know how to speak so bluntly and not sound stupid. 'This is a fantasy.' She gestured with her hand to the view around them. 'This night. This place. You.' She brushed her fingertips over his lips. 'Most especially you.'

He sank slowly beneath the waves pulling her with him until they sat in the shallow water and the warmth of the Jamaican ocean washed over their chests. Her dress clung to her breasts, the nipples hard with desire, and he concentrated all his attention on them. Just the way she liked. Men didn't seem to pay as much attention to breasts any more. But James did. Floating, she wrapped her legs around his waist.

'God, I love the way you respond to my touch.' He tugged her nipples and chuckled when she shivered. 'I could do anything to you, couldn't I? You'd let me do whatever I wanted.'

She moaned, her body on fire.

He lowered his head to her breast, sucking with such force it was almost painful. Gently, he chewed on her nipple through the wet cotton then laved away the sting like a cat with cream.

'Take me to the beach,' she begged. 'Fuck me with your fingers.'

He stood, lifting her easily, and moved on to the beach. 'I bet you don't normally talk like that either, do you?'

Alison turned her head and looked at the resort. Palm trees swayed softly in the evening breeze and the soft strains of reggae floated in the air. It was enchanting. 'Maybe it's this island. But I think it's just you and your magic fingers.'

'Magic fingers,' he murmured, laying her down beyond the surf. 'I like it.' His splayed fingertips moved down from her breasts and tickled her ribcage. He slid down until he lay on his belly in the sand. Urging her thighs apart, he lifted her dripping dress and exposed her to his gaze.

She lay completely exposed while he pleasured her, tasting with his tongue. He was so unabashedly fascinated with the female body and she realised then why he was so successful at making women feel so desirable. It was not the individual woman who appealed to him, but womankind as a whole.

The blunt tip of a finger paused at her opening and she lifted her hips in invitation.

'Breathe in,' he ordered. When she did, her body

sucked the finger inside. Stroking, caressing, he studied her intimately. 'I've wanted to do this for days.' Then he pressed against a secret spot inside her and she jerked in stunned amazement. 'There it is,' he purred in satisfaction and stroked her again. She cried out in pleasure.

'Ah, Alison. I want to touch you all over, fuck you everywhere, hear all the sounds you make.'

'Yes,' she pleaded, falling for his magic touch and sex incarnate voice. It was forbidden, sex with a stranger. Just the thought made her want to come all over his hand.

'All those sessions in the hut,' he whispered. 'Hearing you moan, feeling your body flex and arch under my touch, I almost came in my pants every time. No one's ever been able to arouse me without touching me, without even trying.'

Two fingers entered her, stroking deep inside, moving slowly.

'I'm going to drink all this cream when I'm done, Alison. Will you like that?'

She moaned, riding the edge, so close, hovering. He kept her there deliberately, enjoying her tension, her helplessness.

'Will you like it?' he repeated.

He was torturing her. Well, she could torture right back. 'Almost as much as I'll like drinking you.'

With a groan, his fingers plunged faster. She begged and cursed, bucking up against his hands, loving the feel of being filled and pleasured by his magic fingers. She'd known it would feel like this, wanted his touch, deep inside her. Her hands reached up, pinching her nipples. Lost in the beauty of the island and an attentive man, she came against his hand to the sounds of his low-voiced encouragement.

She woke to sunlight on her face. Her body ached all over, her muscles sore and unwilling to move, still languid with pleasure. Looking at the pillow beside her, she saw that James was gone. She sighed in disappointment. She'd wanted to look at him one last time before she left. Wanted one full lingering look at the hard body that was in such amazing shape it rendered the man tireless.

He'd made love to her all night, just as he'd promised. She hadn't thought it possible that a man could remain hard that long or fill her with desire so many times. She hadn't known a man could talk like he did, with a mesmerising voice and devilish words.

She hadn't known it could hurt so bad to say goodbye to a stranger.

It took her an hour to get into the shower and an hour more to get packed. Despite these delays, it was still all too soon that she stood at the checkout desk and looked over her bill. It was much, much less than it should have been and it took her less than an instant to discover why. In the column of totals, the five massages balanced out to zero.

She stared the paper, her hands shaking. James had whispered, only hours ago, that he should have paid her for the privilege of touching her. She'd thought they were just words, sultry seduction. After all, who'd pay to touch her? But he'd been serious.

Dazed, she signed the register and, before she lost her courage, pulled out her business card and laid it on the counter.

'Please see that James, the masseur, receives this. He expressed an interest in travelling.'

The pretty Jamaican girl behind the counter offered a knowing smile and turned to the small cubicles that lined the wall behind her. She slipped the card in the box labelled 'James' – along with the other dozen that rested there.

Alison smiled sadly and slipped on her sunglasses. There were a few moments left before the shuttle came to take her away from paradise. She moved to the bar and ordered a daiquiri, relishing that tartly sweet taste of strawberries as she strolled to the beach. She kicked off her shoes and stepped on to the sand, her gaze moving past the multitude of sunbathers to the public beach beyond.

Was it only last night that she'd stood in this very spot and wished for a little less loneliness?

She bit the tip of her straw and looked at the massage hut. At this very moment James was working. His hands were gliding over another woman's back, his velvety voice was murmuring coaxing words like a lover would.

The sun beat down and festive music played from the speakers hidden in the palm trees. Guests laughed and enjoyed their holiday. Life went on.

Alison finished her drink and left the empty glass on the bar. It was time to go home.

'You look like you need another holiday.'

Alison looked up from her desk and managed a smile. 'Too much work to do.'

Kathy, her assistant, arched a brow. 'I thought a break would do you good, but you look worse off than when you left.'

She felt worse off. She'd been back at work almost a month now, but it would obviously take longer to get back into the swing of things.

'You look like you haven't slept in days.'

She hadn't. Every time she crawled into bed she thought of James, hard at work with his magic fingers, the Jamaican shore just outside while an aroused woman drowned in the pleasure of his touch.

A hundred times over she wished she'd been more bold, more of a vixen. He'd worked so hard on her, pleasuring her body endlessly, asking nothing in return. She'd loved every moment of it, had thought she would die from the rapture of it. But if she could go back, if she could do it all over again, *she'd* take *him*. She'd pleasure him mindless. She could spend days worshipping his beautiful body.

Impatient fingers snapped in front of her face. 'Hello? Alison?'

Startled, she snapped out of her reverie. 'What?'

'Sleep,' Kathy reiterated. 'You need some sleep.'

'I'm fine. Just a little tense,' she lied, feeling more

so after the arousing mental images she'd just sifted through.

'You need a massage,' purred the deeply masculine voice from the doorway.

Kathy swung round quickly, blocking her view. But Alison didn't need to see to know who it was. Her breath caught.

'Hi,' Kathy called with a come-hither lilt to her voice.

'Hi,' he said softly. 'I just leased the space next door. Thought I'd drop by and introduce myself to my new neighbours.'

Kathy stepped forward, hand outstretched. 'Kathy Martin, travel agent extraordinaire.'

He shook her hand. 'James Mitchell, masseur.'

'Wow. I love massages.' Kathy turned, her eyes wide, obviously smitten. 'This is my boss, Alison.'

Alison pushed back from the desk, her heart racing, her palms sweating. She stepped around Kathy and halted, arrested by the sight of him. Dressed in loose, low-slung jeans and a tight black T-shirt, he was luscious and way too hot to handle.

'I can't believe you're here,' she whispered, afraid to move in case she woke up before they had sex.

His mouth curved wickedly as he moved towards her. His aqua gaze raked her blazer and sundress appreciatively. He stopped a mere inch away, close enough to feel the heat from his skin. He reached down and laced his fingers with hers. 'I thought I'd offer my new neighbour a free massage.'

She melted at his first touch, turned on just from

the scent of him – a heady combination of sex and desire.

'I'm game!' Kathy pitched in.

James chuckled, the warm, rich sound making her nipples ache. His gaze never left hers. 'Stop by in a couple of hours.'

'A couple of hours?' Kathy repeated, finally catching on to the sexual tension that sweltered around them. 'Wow!'

'That's not my usual,' he murmured. 'Alison's special.'

She stared up into his gorgeous face, stunned.

'Ouch!' he muttered with a frown. 'You pinched me.'

'I wanted to see if you were real,' she confessed. 'You're awfully dreamy.'

He laughed and then bent low, his mouth brushing her ear. 'Would I be wrong in thinking you want me to fuck you? Right now?'

'James!' She shivered.

'Would I be wrong, Alison?' he asked again, his shoulder brushing against her hardened nipple, his tongue swiping her earlobe.

She swallowed hard and clutched his hand. 'Yes.'

He paused and arched a brow. 'Really?'

'*I* want to fuck *you*.' And she wasn't embarrassed to say it.

He grinned with approval. 'Let's go.'

Shopping Derby
Heather Towne

Eldon revved the engine. The morning girl from JACK 103 dashed out into the middle of the sun-baked parking lot, chequered flag in hand.

'Stanley's Fine Wine and Spirits Shoppe, corner of Rochester and Marion!' I yelled over the din of the engines and the crowd, and the president of the Chamber of Commerce with a bullhorn. 'Do you know where that is?'

'Yeah!' Eldon responded. 'We're going for the bottle of absinthe first?'

We looked at each other. The guy knew his stores, their merchandise. The government-run liquor outlets didn't carry the Green Fairy, but private wine shops, like Stanley's, did.

I held up my copy of the shopping list that I'd just been handed two minutes earlier. 'I thought we'd knock off the tough stuff first, then mop up the rest in a sprint to the finish.'

Sunlight glinted off Eldon's wire-rimmed glasses, his brown eyes shining. 'I like your style.'

The list quivered in my hand, the excitement and anticipation growing.

The morning girl glanced nervously at the ten seventeen-foot U-Haul cube trucks assembled in front of her, motors running, then at the Chamber of Commerce guy safely ensconced in the portable stands packed with shopkeepers and curious onlookers.

'On your marks!' the president bullhorned.

Truck horns blared.

'Get set!'

Engines revved.

'Shop!'

We were off, lumbering across the parking lot, a converging line of rumbling cargo vehicles headed for the industrial park exit roads. The Shopping Derby was on.

Each truck contained a man and a woman – ten teams randomly formed from the twenty people randomly selected out of the hundreds of applicants to compete – a map of the city, a book of Yellow Pages, and the shopping list of one hundred items we were supposed to purchase in twelve hours or less. Cellphones, BlackBerries and any other type of store-communication device were banned. The contest was a test of shopping skills and stamina, knowledge of the city and its stores and their wares; the results judged on price and quality, as well as quantity.

We were at the head of the thundering pack when we hit the first traffic light that led to the city proper, careful to obey all traffic regulations and speed limits as required, of course. An Air-JACK helicopter hovered over our heads, monitoring the race.

'What's after the absinthe?' Eldon asked.

Planning ahead – good. I was way ahead of him, though, prioritising items with my ballpoint based on purchasing difficulty and probable store location, seeking the coveted cluster effect to cut down on travel time. 'A purple leather bustier,' I answered. 'I'm pretty sure the Underwear Drawer on Clarence carries purple ones – at a reasonable price.'

Eldon brushed his brown hair over to the right and glanced at me. 'Don't just be pretty, be sure.'

I got a good feeling he and I were going places.

We watched Trucks 4 and 7 steam off to the right down the four-lane street.

'Wal-Mart,' we said together, shaking our heads. They had a big box two blocks to the west.

Most of the items on the shopping list weren't the usual generic junk you buy at a big department store, however. What skill does that take? But there were some; the easy stuff, worth less points in the grand scheme of things.

The light stayed red, taunting us.

'You know the city pretty well?' I asked, phone book and map bouncing up and down in my lap, in time with my legs.

Eldon drummed the steering wheel and said, 'Drove a cab before I got my CGA.'

The light changed at last, and we chugged off into traffic, eastbound, both of us scanning the horizon for bottlenecks. The clock was ticking.

'What do you do for a living?' Eldon asked, checking the rear-view mirror the recommended every ten seconds.

I was zipping through the shopping list for the

fifth time. 'Huh? Oh, I'm a purchaser for Coachways – the bus manufacturer.' Not that that was going to be of any help. All the items on the list were personal products – housewares, clothing, health goods, sporting equipment, kids' stuff – not industrial components.

'Go!' Eldon hollered at me, rocking to a stop in front of Stanley's Fine Wine and Spirits Shoppe. The place had just opened; timing is everything during a shopping binge.

I dashed out of the truck and into the store, telling the man sporting the 'Stanley' nametag exactly what I wanted, loud and clear. Communication is critical in getting the right product, quickly.

He waddled around the pub-style counter and plucked a dusty bottle off a wall shelf, then glanced at the idling truck out front. Eldon was already in the street with the rear doors open, ready to load.

'Shopping derby, eh?' Stanley commented. He casually scratched his salt-and-pepper beard with the bottle top. 'Great idea by the Chamber. I got in as a sponsor on that one right off the bat. I knew it would get loads of publicity. What're you and your partner going to do with the ten thousand if you –'

'Just bag the bottle, Stan,' I gritted.

I flew out of the store, tossed the booze up to Eldon in the back of the truck. He dropped it in a cardboard box, then jumped out, as I slid behind the wheel. We were off.

Traffic was picking up, along with the heat. I hugged the outside lane, keeping things rolling. My heart was pumping a mile a minute, and so, apparently, was Eldon's.

'Buy a lot of stuff at the Underwear Drawer?'

'On occasion,' I said. 'Like any naughty girl.'

We looked at each other.

I made the kerb in front of the lingerie and sex toy emporium in five minutes, then leapt out and scooted inside. I knew just where to go – and not from studying flyers, ad bags, store layouts, websites, or the Yellow Pages, either.

I spotted the rack of leather bustiers near the rear of the store and started flipping. The rich aroma and texture made me a little dizzy. Black, black, black, red, red, white ... no purple!

I made tracks for the green-haired clerk behind the cash register. 'Don't you carry any purple leather bustiers, Nancy? Size medium.'

She fluttered her false eyelashes as I clawed the countertop. 'Well, um ... if you don't, like, see any on display ... we might, um, have some –'

'Get one!'

She dropped the crotchless panties she'd been pricing and scurried off to the storeroom. One of the many things this competition was going to test, was how well you handled the hired help.

She was back in under a minute with my leather bustier, right colour, right size. I fingered the requisite bills off Eldon's and my combined roll and handed them to her. You had to pay your own way in the derby – that was the entrance fee. Only the winners would be reimbursed. Thriftiness was important, therefore, as it always is with any good shopper.

I grabbed the bagged bawdywear and sailed outside. Eldon was in the cargo cube, bent over arranging boxes and padded mats, preparing. His hard buttocks roundly filled the rear of his tan Dockers. Sweat rolled down my back and into my shorts.

He spun around. I threw him the bag. He boxed it and jumped down out of the truck, colliding with me. My breasts bounced off his chest, stunning me, thrilling me. And impulsively (so unlike the way I shopped), I grabbed the guy's head between my hands and kissed him.

The frenzy was getting to me, I guess.

We stared at one another. Then he pushed me back and bolted for the cab of the truck. Still, even as he ran away, I sensed a connection deeper than commerce between the two of us.

World Cup Germany soccer ball – Kick It! on Gertrude, the store adjoining the new indoor soccer facility. It paid to read the newspapers, which Eldon did scrupulously.

This time I flung the cargo doors open while my partner raced into the store. He was out with pace in a matter of seconds, a silver Adidas soccer ball bearing the 2006 World Cup logo in his hands. He kicked it up to me where I stood on the edge of the truckbed, along with the comment, 'Nice legs.'

The pale-pink shorty-shorts I was wearing for action *did* do a good job of showing off my long legs. Two-mile daily jogs had turned them summer lean and brown.

'Thanks,' I said, jumping down.

He caught me, kissed me. His lips were soft and

slightly wet. He darted his tongue into my mouth, tussled with my tongue, and a tingle shot through me. I broke away, damp and breathless and even more pumped for the hunt.

I slid behind the wheel and gunned the engine.

'They should have a Fat Boy barbecue at Grillers on Fort Street,' he said, scanning the shopping list from the passenger seat.

'Thought so,' I muttered, strangling the steering wheel, his warm hand riding my bare thigh.

We squeezed into the alley next to the barbecue store; there was no parking on the street. Eldon ran inside while I flopped the rear doors open. Then I thought about the size and weight of that jumbo propane cooking apparatus, and I started after him.

But he was already back at the mouth of the alley, a store clerk guiding one end of the rolling barbecue, hustling to keep up. Good help wasn't hard to find, once you demanded it.

The two men heaved the grill into the back while I fidgeted behind the wheel. The doors finally slammed shut and Eldon slid in next to me. We rolled.

'Does the Constantine Nursery on Shell carry that type of fern?' I asked, pointing at the jumping list in his hand. My finger slipped, poking him in the stomach. He was hard under his conservative green golf shirt, and ribbed.

Eldon shook his head, sweat beading his tall forehead. 'I doubt it. Their inventory is mainly flowers – annuals and perennials and the like. They don't carry many non-flowering plants. Green-thumbs on Cavalier has plenty of plants, though.'

I nodded, grinning. 'I knew there was a reason I brought you along.'

I rode the rear of a Smart car until it jittered off into another lane.

The Greenthumbs on Cavalier was closed. Eldon spotted that two blocks away. I hung a U-turn and headed for their other location on Adelaide. I was shaking again – not with nervousness, with excitement.

The second Greenthumbs was open. We both piled out of the truck. Large greenhouses are notorious for scattering their living wares all over God's half-acre, staff often as difficult to find as marigolds in January. So four legs would be better than two, in this case.

I located the fern section first, the plant we were seeking peeking out from behind a mini-forest of its scruffier cousins. We carefully loaded the greenery into the truck.

Then I pushed Eldon against a side panel, pressing my lips into his, my overheated body against his body. It was a sauna in the back of that truck, but we were already too sweaty to care. We swirled our tongues together, Eldon's hands sliding down my back and onto my bum. He gripped and squeezed my taut little buns, his erection pressing hard and yearningly against my stomach. I moaned into his mouth, fingers riffling his hair.

We broke apart in unison.

'*History of Canada, 1497 to 1750, The Years of Discovery*, Jock Miller?' I gasped.

'University Bookstore, for sure,' he exhaled. 'But that's way over on the edge of town.'

'Used bookstore?' I snapped, clutching his shoulders.

'Yeah,' he agreed, almost cracking a smile as he stared at my rapidly rising and falling breasts. 'The Learned Worm on Florence. They carry used textbooks. At least they did when I –'

'Let's go,' I hissed, shutting him up with a kiss.

By hour six we had fifty-two items crossed off our shopping list, snug in the back of our truck. The JACK guys in the chopper informed us over the radio that three trucks had already been ticketed and one towed. And two other trucks were running fine, but their passengers had broken down – screaming at one another on the sidewalk as they hopelessly floundered. Long-haul shopping can wear on the nerves of the best of companions. Especially when you don't know what you're doing.

We knew what we were doing. Each item purchased, checked off our list, was rewarded with a hug or a kiss or a grope, or all three, depending on the pertinent parking circumstances. We were brimming with adrenalin, the finish line and prize money in sight; turned on rather than tired out.

'Romeo Busante hand-dipped chocolates, dark, twelve pieces in a heart-shaped box!' Eldon called out to me over the roar of the road.

I swiped perspiration off my forehead and smiled. 'A girl's best friend. Better Than Sex, Waterfront Drive.'

He squeezed my leg. I puckered a pretend kiss.

It was almost cool in the little stand of trees in the park behind the Waterfront Shopping Center, what with the shade and the breeze from the lake. But not for Eldon and me.

He was on top of me, cupping my breasts through my damp T-shirt, licking my nipples. I shimmered with delight, staring up at the fluffy clouds drifting by on the brilliantly blue sky, the box of Busante's resting comfortably on the grass next to us.

'Yes,' I urged, when he closed his lips over a rigid clothed bud and sucked on it, flooding me with even more heat.

He bathed my T-shirted breasts with his tongue, sucking and biting my nipples, before finally pushing my top up and baring my boobs. I flung my arms over my head and arched my back, begging the earnest accountant to ravage my chest.

He grasped and squeezed my slippery breasts, flicking a cherry-red nipple still harder and higher with his tongue, the dizzying tingling sensation driving me wild. I twisted my head around in the grass, and he pushed my tits together, slashing his tongue across the stiffened peaks of both of them at once. I closed my eyes, my body vibrating.

He mauled and sucked on my breasts until, finally, I grabbed his head and brought him up to my mouth, my pussy as wet as the lake.

'We should really hit the road,' he said, foggy glasses riding his forehead.

The guy sure knew how to tease a girl. But that could be forgiven, even encouraged, because he sure knew how to shop.

I rolled over on top of him, our lips locked together. Then I levered a hand in between our flaming bodies and covered the hardened outline of his cock with a warm palm. I squeezed and rubbed him, and he moaned into my mouth, throbbing in my hand.

'Yes, I suppose we really should hit the road,' I breathed, rolling off of him.

I brushed grass out of my hair and pulled out my T-shirt in an effort to dry it, as Eldon shifted into gear.

'Dungeons and Dragons Howling Orc miniature, War Drums set?'

'The Sorcerer's Apprentice and Sons, on Euclid,' he replied instantly.

I touched his arm. He goosed the gas.

We weren't the only ones to find the mouldering storefront sepulchre of geekdom, however; the Truck 8 contestants were there ahead of us, though still far behind us in the overall race. The woman was arguing with an H.P. Lovecraft lookalike behind the counter, brandishing a shopping list that showed only about twenty checkmarks.

'You've got to have this stupid troll!' she wailed, shoving the list in H.P.'s face. Her braided brown hair was coming apart at the seams, the back of her neck a blistered red.

Her partner, a pale pudgy guy with a goatee, stood next to her, shoulders hunched, rocking back and forth, lips moving as if in silent prayer. His glassy eyes and demeanour were testimony to a terminal case of shopping stress.

'Madam, it is an Orc, not a troll,' H.P. intoned, folding his parchment fingers together. 'And, as I have already explained to you, I had, unfortunately, but two of that particular miniature, both of which have been purchased from me in the last hour. Perhaps you may obtain one at −'

But the woman wasn't listening, she was screaming, tearing at her hair, her companion rocking faster.

We exited, beelining for Dougie's Black Hole at the Springside Mall. One thing every experienced, time-wary shopper knows: you don't argue with store staff − either they have what you want, or they don't. And if they don't, you move on.

We scooped up the figurine and then wrestled with each other in the cab of the truck, Eldon's busy hands shopping for purchase on my most private of possessions. The vying for buying supremacy had thrown us together, and brought us together, our passion building alongside our cargo, the heat of battle inflaming us to take chances we'd never take outside of an all-out shopping derby.

'TanFan burnt-orange paisley dress, extra large,' I stated, after Eldon had stored the Greek-language Nana Mouskouri CD from Second Sound Sensations in the back. 'There's a vintage clothing store on Marlborough.'

'Why vintage?' he asked.

'TanFan went out of business right after Chip & Pepper.'

He cracked a smile.

Traffic was heavy, but I drafted in behind a bus, and we were hanging a right onto Marlborough in the time it took most people to tear open their credit card bill. Eldon followed me into the funky boutique. I didn't ask why; I knew why. I was going to try on the dress even though it was unnecessary, and too large, and he was going to help.

I stripped off my sticky T-shirt in the crowded curtained change booth, Eldon dropping to his knees in front of me. He unbuttoned and unzipped my shorts, yanked them down, leaving me bare, bottom and top. My legs shook and my arms goosebumped as he ran his warm hands up and down my legs. And when he ran them up over the swell of my buttocks, and gripped my cheeks, I squeaked.

His breath steamed hot and humid against my moist naked sex. I wrung the paisley dress in my damp hands. He let slip his tongue and licked me, and I almost tore the threadbare garment to threads.

'Jesus, yes,' I whimpered, leaning back against the wall, the man's tongue caressing my lips.

He held me by the bum and lapped at me, sending me shivering. I discarded the dress and grabbed onto his hair, pulling him into my dewy need. A heavy languid heat consumed me as he wriggled his tongue inside of me, and I gasped to fill my lungs in the suddenly breathless confines. And when he spread me apart and flicked at my button, I just about melted in the man's mouth.

I had to put a stop to it, for the good of the team. I just couldn't take any more. And I wanted physical culmination to come with contest culmination, as I knew he did, too.

So I jerked his head back, bent down and kissed him on his shiny lips. I helped him to his feet, then spun him around and tried *him* on for size.

Taking his spot on the floor, I unzipped his pants and pulled him hard and needful out into the open. The merchandise was just as advertised, and I admired it with my soft swirling hand, testing and teasing its length and strength. I took his swollen head into my warm wet mouth, then half his shaft.

'Fuck,' he groaned, startling me with the curse word.

I gripped his thickened base and bobbed my head, lips sliding back and forth on his pulsing manhood, tongue cushioning the veiny underside. I cupped his pouch as I sucked, squeezing and tugging.

'That's enough! That's enough!' he cried, grabbing at my bangs.

I pulled him out of my mouth with a soggy pop, the both of us very much on edge.

Four hours later, ten hours in, there was only one item left on our shopping list: a fold-out futon. We weren't cocky, but we had a good warm feeling that we were well ahead of the rest of the field. And even if some of our competition managed to somehow buy all one hundred items, we were confident we could beat them on quality and price.

'The Futon Factory on Bishop?' I asked, cradling the Yellow Pages, balancing the map in my lap.

'Sure, if you want to pay full price. But when I was monitoring local TV commercials this past month, I'm sure I saw an Al's Unpainted Furnishings spot advertising a sale on just that product. Wanna give it a try?'

He looked at me just a little smugly, and I could've kissed him. Did, in fact, right on the dimpled chin. 'You haven't been wrong yet,' I said.

He spun the wheel to the left, and ten minutes later we were in the gargantuan parking lot of the Al's Unpainted Furnishings warehouse on Clairemont. 'Shellacless' Al, owner and star of a hundred annoying TV advertisements, was there to greet us on the cavernous showroom floor.

We told him what we were after. He said he had it, but we'd have to get it. Al had rock-bottom prices, and customer service to match.

Eldon and I lugged the futon out of the store and into the glaring sunlight, heaved it aboard the truck. It was hot heavy work, but we were so keyed up we hardly took notice. We stood in the back of the truck, amongst our one hundred prescribed and purchased items, panting with exhilaration. Then Eldon shoved me down onto the futon.

He closed the cargo doors to only a crack, felt for me, found me, ready and willing. I pulled him down on top of me, his hard body fitting neatly against mine, the discount futon creaking, but standing its ground. He kissed my lips, my nose, my neck, licked and bit into my neck. I wrapped my arms and legs around him and nuzzled his hair. His tongue trailed up over my chin, into my waiting mouth.

It was dark in that giant shopping cart, but a sliver of light and a previous familiarity with each other's bodies showed us the way. No words were exchanged. There was nothing to say now, just do. We might be finicky shoppers, but we knew what we liked.

Eldon rolled my T-shirt up over my breasts and fingered my achingly hard nipples. He took them in his mouth, each in turn, sucking on them, as I clawed my shorts and panties down, my head spinning. He released my breasts long enough to strip out of his own pants and underwear. Then he was on top of me again, sliding inside of me at last.

I grasped his bare bum as he pumped me, sweat streaming off his face and onto mine, his searching tongue swarming into my mouth. He clung to my quivering breasts and I clung to his clenching buttocks, his hips moving faster and faster, filling me with sensuous joy.

I started to shake, my body a live wire, a wicked tingling blazing up from the wet-hot friction point where we were joined, where Eldon pistoned away. A scream caught in my throat. He threw back his head and grunted. I shuddered, he jerked, the inferno of our ecstasy engulfing us. I flooded with wave after wave of warm wet delight, as he emptied himself inside of me.

We collected the ten thousand dollar prize money, all right, and were reimbursed for our purchases (which we got to keep). The next closest couple only managed to muster a measly 86 rather overpriced items.

But we didn't go running out shopping for engagement rings, or starter houses, or anything like that. Eldon was married, after all, as was I.

We'd come together for a brief encounter during the madness of the derby, sharing our passion for purchasing. But now that the buying spree was over, we returned to our families.

I got custody of the futon.

Heather Towne's short stories have appeared in numerous Wicked Words collections.

Her Brush Jill Bannelec

I have my own business and I am my own boss. I work when I need to, and I get to pick and choose who I work for. Before you jump to conclusions, what I do is legal. I trained hard for it. I was the only girl in that year's intake at the technical college, and I was ready for the jibes from the others – school leavers like myself, but who were all male. I was the exception, the girl apprentice in a class of 25 blokes, but I wanted to be just what they did – a painter and decorator.

It was a hard slog, which I had anticipated, especially the plastering, but my being there also seemed to make it difficult for my fellow students. Some of the guys seemed distracted by my presence and were unable to concentrate, some even blaming me for their failings with calculations and wallpaper hanging as their eyes wandered to my curvy shape – even clad in regulation blue overalls. And in the warm early autumn days at the start of the course, I must admit that I sometimes popped a button or two open for air as I was grafting hard, stretching and pasting and wielding paper strippers and planes.

The teacher, Ron, announced that no one should treat me differently, equal opps and all that, but it didn't stop them trying it on. I'm an OK looker, so

I'm told, and had even once considered modelling as an alternative career. But despite what the tutor had said, nobody took me seriously, even though I'd made a good start, and those I told to sod off when they tried it on told the rest I was a lesbian. Typical. Why else would I want a man's job?

To be honest, Ron probably fancied a go at me from the day he saw my name on the register. He was twice my age but very fit, and because I showed enthusiasm he took me under his wing, although, inevitably, the conversations between us got a little fruity as time went on. I remember his politically correct behaviour slowly morphing into oh so predictable male patter, and also how we eventually had sex on his desk after the final evening class.

'Don't forget what I've taught you,' he said, climbing on top of me as a pile of paint charts dug into my back. 'Dip your brush in about two-thirds of its length; wipe the surplus off as it leaves the tin, and commence long generous strokes until it's empty.'

Some of the lads dropped out of the course but I stayed, mastering the theory as well as the practical, blistering my fingers, breaking my nails, and getting the odd gloop of paint in my shoulder-length dark hair. I studied hard, ignored the quips and the gropes, and was rewarded by finally getting my articles and venturing forth as a time-served craftsperson, being eventually accepted onto the council decorating team as 'one of the lads'.

After that, I thought I had it all under control until the day we lost a contract and I found myself redundant at 25 with a mortgage around my neck. I'd invested in a small terraced cottage and, of course, redecorated it myself. It seemed a good idea at the time. Unfortunately, one of the first things people do to save a bit of money when things get tough is to put things off, and those things, I found to my cost, always included decorating. But then I had my brainwave.

I advertised as a fully qualified 'lady decorator', a concept I thought might appeal to single women who didn't want cowboys – although there could, of course, be such a thing as a cowgirl – but, more importantly, who felt safer with a member of the same sex working in their home. It was an instant success, and I was soon overwhelmed with work from elderly ladies and career girls to single mums. I was even able to be generous when I thought they couldn't afford my normal rates, and found myself the subject of an article in the local press, complete with photographs of myself in and out of dungarees. It praised my enterprise and entrepreneurial skills, and brought in even more business. I bought myself a van, with my business name, 'Her Brush', boldly emblazoned on the side, and settled down to a lifestyle that I had dreamed of, managing my hours to include plenty of time off for riding during the summer, and keeping the interior work for the cold, wet days of winter.

And then, after the article appeared, so did the other possibilities of my apparently unique service, ones that had never previously occurred to me. Men also started to ring for quotations and estimates. Some were obnoxious, some obviously on the pull, and some sounded genuine, but the truth was I didn't need their work. I put the first few off, saying I had too much on but, eventually, I thought, Why not? I might even meet someone fanciable; be a bit of a cheeky chappess on the job. It had been a while since I had met a kindred spirit, but it never entered my head that they might be married, or a bit odd. If I didn't like the look of a caller, I thought, I could always give an inflated estimate but, if I did fancy him, he might even get it at trade cost. I decided to give it a try, conscious that the customer's motive for choosing an attractive woman to decorate their bedroom might involve more than the usual required tasks of a painter and decorator. So what, I decided. So what?

In the late summer, just when I was on the lookout for a nice lucrative interior job during the cooler days, it happened. Out of the blue, a guy called Josh Ettersby rang from Roland Towers, a select office block that had been built in the late 80s as part of the revitalisation of the former docks area of the city. It was nearly ten miles from my house, but I knew the area was renowned for successful small businesses and Josh sounded quite nice for a budding millionaire. Besides, I might be his neighbour one day, so I needed to check the place out.

I finished early for the day, got changed and took the lift up to the fifteenth floor, taking in the view of the shimmering, sunlit waters surrounding the building, and opened the door bearing the gold lettering: 'J. Ettersby – Actuary'. I looked across the room to see the smiling face of a rather conservatively dressed woman, probably in her early thirties, whom I took to be his secretary.

'Ms Carpenter?' she asked, standing up and offering her hand. I nodded, recognising the standard City uniform of white blouse and regulation-length dark skirt. She beckoned me in. 'I'm Sally Jones, Mr Ettersby's PA. He's expecting you. He thinks you're quite a celebrity, breaking the mould, so to speak. It must have taken a lot of bottle.'

I was thrown by the unexpected praise. 'I suppose it did,' I replied, 'but I just didn't see myself working in an office like all...' I heard my voice trail away as I realised I was being less than diplomatic, but luckily she didn't seem to mind.

'I know what you mean,' she said, generously putting me at ease, 'but it has its rewards.' She sat down, swivelling her chair back under her desk and smoothing her skirt under her thighs. She seemed to take an age, and I was sure she deliberately gave me a glimpse of her cleavage as she leaned forwards to speak to me about the job. I did a double take; our eyes met, and there was an uneasy silence for a moment or two as hers challenged mine. I was saved as Josh Ettersby came out of his office.

'Hello,' he said, offering his hand. 'You must be Ms Carpenter.' I'll never forget his firm, yet gentle, grip on my hand. He was gorgeous, and I immediately wanted this job more than any other I'd taken on. He was about my age, well built, with a mass of blond hair flopping across his forehead, and wearing an immaculate dark-grey suit. He even smelled good. I felt his gaze and also Ms Jones's stare settling on me, and my breathing quickened as my emotions struggled with the unexpected situation. 'Come and see what you think,' he said, beckoning me in to his office.

The room was large, filled with a deep rich crimson carpet. One side was taken up with a picture window that afforded a spectacular view over the water below. His large mahogany desk seemed somewhat old-fashioned, with its inlaid bottle-green leather top, massive intricately carved legs and heavy brass handles on the numerous drawers but, if an actuary couldn't have a desk like that, then who could? On top of it sat a laptop and an intercom that doubled as a phone. A row of wooden filing cabinets and an oak bookcase filled the opposite wall, and a table and six chairs matching the desk occupied the space under the window. Behind the desk was another door, slightly ajar, to reveal what appeared to be a shower cubicle.

Josh waited until I had assuaged my curiosity before speaking.

'I wanted a look that combined modernity with quality and tradition, if that isn't a contradiction in terms,' he said. 'My clients like the idea of security and lasting values, but recognise the need for me to invest their hard-gotten gains with some element of risk if they are to be successful. The interior designer came up with these.' He handed me some colour samples – emulsion, gloss and stains – and some very expensive-looking wallpaper.

'What do you think?'

I studied them, and in my mind's eye applied them to the room, nodding in appreciation.

'What's your opinion?' he asked, smiling.

The opinion I was forming at that very moment was unlikely to be the one he had in mind. It was of him sitting on the corner of his desk, pants drawn tightly across his muscular thighs, arms casually folded across his chest. And it was very obvious that he dressed on the left.

'I think it will be very attractive,' I said, actually liking the designer's work, and trying to avoid staring at his crotch. 'But what about the room opposite?'

'No. That's OK. It's just the loo and shower. I go jogging straight after work, so it's useful to have somewhere to get changed and freshen up. Anyway, do your measuring up while I get changed, 'cos it's jogging time right now.' He strode out with an energetic bounce, closing the door behind him, and I set to work trying not to think about him stripping off a few feet away. I tried to concentrate on the real reason I was there, but the close proximity of the vivacious young actuary had succeeded in making me seriously aroused as I entertained notions of inappropriate behaviour that I was obliged to quickly suppress for the sake of my income.

He emerged while I was crouching behind the table, measuring the window, and I had a perfect vantage point to give his lower body a surreptitious once-over as he re-entered the room. He was wearing a snazzy pair of lightweight trainers, a vest top and some expensive designer shorts, every inch the young executive at play, and this look had an even more marked effect on my desire to see what was underneath. I straightened up, fighting the urge once more to look at his crotch, his cock coiled and bulging in his groin, probably aching to be caressed. His face betrayed not a hint of self-consciousness as he casually walked out. 'See you later,' he said. 'Give Sally a shout when you're finished.'

I left, reluctantly, before he returned, my fertile imagination working overtime as I drove home. I worked hard over the next few days, pitching the price as low as I dared, and hoping that any profit would be physical rather than fiscal. The following week we met again, and he and Sally pronounced themselves more than happy with my references and estimate. The only complication was that the job had to be finished within a fortnight, and I had to work between five and eight each night, when Josh had finished in his office. I made a start the next day, being left to my own devices after Sally had gone home and Josh was out for his daily jog.

When he returned that first evening, still perspiring as he let himself in, I couldn't resist the urge to study him as I sanded the paintwork, dressed in my blue overalls but cheekily wearing only the finest lingerie underneath, just in case he was overpowered by passion for his painter and decorator. Like, yeah, dream on, girl, I thought. His muscular legs were covered in a sheen of sweat, and an intoxicating muskiness filled the room. He peeled his T-shirt over his broad shoulders just enough to give me a tempting flash of his body as he disappeared into the shower room without even a backward glance.

I listened to him singing in the shower and cursing as the soap periodically clanged to the floor of the cubicle. In my imagination, he was thinking of me as he washed himself, using more than enough soap as he handled his cock and lathered it up, which hardened as he fantasised of how one day he would tell Ms Jones to cancel all calls and appointments so that he could concentrate on me. We would do it on the desk and then shower together, making love a second time in the steamy, slippery heat. My fingers were already delving under the side buttons of my overalls and into my coffee-coloured, lace-trimmed satin panties. There was something so decadent about wearing such girlie fabrics underneath the industrial cloth of the overalls. I was being so unprofessional, but it was so hard not to think of the floppy-haired Josh. How I wished I was holding the soap and not my dusty sandpapering block, as I laboriously prepared the woodwork and filled the cracks in the plaster. I heard the water stop, then he emerged, drying his hair with one towel, another around his waist. I looked away, a mixture of lust and embarrassment in my mind. How could he torture me so?

Over the coming week, we exchanged the usual platitudes about the weather and about my unusual choice of career. He was very pleasant and had lovely manners, but I could see that his mind began to wander after a few moments of hearing my 'tales of a painter and decorator'; no girlfriend of his would have such a lowly occupation, I'm sure. It just wouldn't be right, and certainly not feminine. But things were to take a curious turn by the end of that week. One evening, when he had left after his shower, I deftly applied the posh paper that had been delivered that afternoon to one of the walls and took a sneaky few minutes of relaxation and reward, reclining in his luxury leather desk chair, breathing in its delicious scent as I spun around like a kid. I even played with the buttons on the intercom, mimicking his voice.

'Bring me a coffee, Ms Jones, and then lean over the desk while I shag you from behind. No. On second thoughts, bring that decorator woman with you. I fancy a change.' I allowed my imagination free rein now that I was alone. If he could see and hear what I got up to – that as my arousal built to such a peak I brought myself off in his shower while I rubbed his still-warm shorts between my legs – he would have had a heart attack, but that was exactly what I was doing when the phone rang.

I ignored it at first, then realised he just might be checking up on me. I dashed for the desk and flicked the switch.

'I'm glad you know how to work the thing. It took me weeks,' said Josh. 'You sound out of breath. I must be working you too hard. Anyway, I wondered if you fancied something to eat.' I tried to control my breathing as I squatted out of sight from the other buildings and dripped all over the dust sheets. I did my best to mask the excitement in my voice, trying to sound as nonchalant as possible.

'OK, thanks, but I'm up to my neck in it right now. Give me twenty minutes. Where shall I meet you?' I stuttered.

'Actually I was thinking of a takeaway. Chinese? Good. I'll get their special deal. I'll see you there in ten minutes.'

I sat there for a second or two in a nervous puddle, but as I shakily stood up I jogged the keyboard of his computer and activated the screen. And that was how I found his pictures.

He had a folder of JPEGS of a woman in various states of arousal. The first depicted her in a dishevelled but smart office skirt and blouse on all fours looking up at the bulging crotch of an otherwise unseen man. Her skirt was rucked up to her waist, and her long tanned legs were finished off by a pair of ankle boots. She had no underwear on and her naked backside was facing the camera, giving an embarrassingly pin-sharp, glorious view of her exposed and swollen, glistening cunt.

I was speechless staring at it, finding it shocking that such a well-mannered young man had such filthy tastes. I clicked on another JPEG, my heart beating wildly as I wondered what it would reveal. This was taken from the same shoot; an obviously excited male was on all fours, his hard cock pointing at a crimson carpet. The woman was on offer and he was ready to mount her, like an animal. I felt my own excitement building. I'm not innocent or inexperienced, and certainly not prudish, but this was something else. I realised who the people in the photographs must be – Josh Ettersby and the prim, efficient, conservative Ms Jones! My horror turned to excitement and then jealousy as I studied the rest. They were in some sort of chronological order, oral sex on him, several featuring penetration, and ending with Josh coming all over Sally's face and breasts. I had suddenly become hot, sweating in the air-conditioned room. I caught sight of myself in a mirror, noticing that my nipples were hard and peaked, my chest flushed with excitement. I squeezed one nipple gently, and one thing led to another. My right hand slid back between my legs, slipping into my warm, pungent wetness.

As I gazed at the last photograph, my envy for Ms Jones and the power she was able to exert over Josh became a flame of jealousy, and my fingers were frantic over my clit. Ms Jones's sex lips were parted, her splayed legs high in the air, her knees bent like a cat waiting to be tickled. She had a pleading but knowing expression on her face, as if confident of getting just what she was begging for, which she did, as it sprayed over her. It pushed me over the edge and, as I fixed the image in my mind's eye, I came, chest heaving, hips bucking, reeling on the floor with the aftershocks of an intense orgasm. I dropped down onto my haunches, panting uncontrollably, taken by surprise by the strength of my arousal and the intensity of my response. And then I remembered Josh was just a few moments away.

I clicked the photographs to close into the folder, then went into the shower room, my thighs damp with the honeyed juices of my ecstasy. I soaped myself clean, feeling invigorated and almost opiated by the endorphins that rushed through my body, and I dressed in a guilty silence, wondering how I would look Josh in the eye, then I heard his key in the lock, and he wandered in.

'Very nice,' he said glancing at the one wall that I had managed to finish. 'The paper looks really good.' I smiled at the praise, but he saw there was something else in my expression. 'Anything wrong?' he asked with seemingly genuine concern.

My thoughts returned to the images. I stuttered an unconvincing, 'No.'

'Why don't you call it a night?' he suggested. 'You look like you've been overdoing it. It's nearly seven. I'll unpack the Chinese.' The food smelled delicious, and I was hungry after my earlier expelling of energy.

'Thanks,' I said, regaining some composure at last, and thinking I'd got away with it. 'I think I will.'

I tidied up as he unpacked the meal and laid it out on the desk, complete with a bottle of red wine. He brought a chair over for himself and insisted I use his. He adjusted the height for me, hopefully not realising I had moved it only a few minutes before, and slid it under my bottom as I sat down, ever the perfect gentleman, but one with a secret, whom I now saw in a far different light. We ate steadily, the wine excellent and the food delicious. There was a continuing heat between my legs that confirmed my desire to be part of the fantasy. I gradually relaxed as the wine hit me and there seemed to be less chance of me being found out. Then he spoke.

'Just click on that photo file on the desktop, will

you,' he said, so matter of factly, but so devastat-
ingly, nodding at the laptop. What could I do?
Refuse? How, without letting the cat out of the
bag? I tentatively opened it up, turning the laptop
to face him.

'What did you think of them?' he asked quietly,
standing up and walking behind my chair, ''cos I
know you've been peeking.' He spun it round then
so that I faced him, but I stared at the floor as if I
were guilty of something appallingly rude and, for
an instant, I thought of denying it, but the shame
and arousal in my eyes told a different story.

'Your silence tells me all that I need to know,' he
said, crestfallen. 'I'm so sorry if I've upset you, Jane,
but I had to know.' It was the first time he had
called me by my Christian name, and I suppressed
a shiver, but I detected a genuine concern and self-
doubt in his voice as he spoke.

I still couldn't look him in the eye, but heard
myself say, quietly but clearly, 'I found them ...
exciting. I can't believe that you would have pictures like that; they're so explicit.'

Then there was a long, torturous pause before I
spilled out what I really felt, that I wished the
woman was me and not Ms Jones. Afterwards, I
was genuinely relieved that I had managed to say
what I really wanted to, but I felt a different
tension blossom in the room. I knew a business
relationship had just moved into uncharted waters,
and I feared for what would happen. Would I lose
the contract? Dare I show such unprofessional com-
plicity in his pervy hobby? Would he want me to
get involved or not? Slowly, I looked up at his face,

to see the expression of a child who has just unwrapped the one Christmas present he really wanted. He refilled the wineglasses and gave mine to me.

'A toast,' he said, 'to naughty fun in private rooms! You are sure you liked them?'

I nodded, my expression slowly mirroring his.

He then opened his briefcase, took out some printed photographs, and handed them to me. They were stills from a CCTV, of relatively poor quality but quite clearly photographs of me. In the first one I was hard at work, in the second I was sat on the floor of his shower room with his shorts held up to my face; and in the third I was bringing myself off with them pressed between my legs. I felt myself blushing with a mixture of anger, indignation and renewed arousal.

'I take it I'm off the job?' I said, my voice wavering with emotion.

'No. No. Not at all,' he said. 'In fact, it's you "on the job" that I like to see. You see, most of the porn I like features smartly dressed women, or them wearing kinky stuff – the predictable whips and corsets. I like women to look a bit tougher, I suppose. Women in uniform and –' he hesitated '– work wear. Overalls and kind of butch stuff. I like girls who don't mind getting messy.'

I was surprised and puzzled, but there was no anger in his voice, only anticipation. I opened my mouth to speak, only to be silenced by his finger firmly against my lips. I knew better than to refuse.

'I like what you wear,' he continued. 'All the time you were telling me about your painting and decorating antics I had a raging hard-on. I was thinking about you naked under those overalls. It would be so easy to pop the metal buttons and grab you!'

The pasting table was still out and, with shaking hands, I measured a new piece of paper, cut it to size, and laid it out ready for pasting. Josh motioned to the table.

'Go on, let me see you hard at it,' he said, his voice thick with anticipation.

I picked up the broad brush and dipped it deeply into the plastic bowl full of paste, for once not automatically remembering Ron's advice as I began to spread it evenly over the paper. As I leaned across it, making sure the far edge was generously covered, I heard him close the window blinds, then I sensed him directly behind me.

'Don't stop, Ms Carpenter,' he said, slipping his hands around my waist and then up to where the overalls were buttoned down the front. 'I want to capture you on film as you work, but these are not for the local paper, they are just for me. Is that all right with you?' The implications of this were huge, but I felt myself nodding as the words left his mouth. 'Right. Just carry on, ignore the camera.' I tried to concentrate, recharging the brush, as he slowly popped each button until the overalls were baggy on me and my sexy lingerie was exposed, to which he gave a knowing cry of delight. Down they went, over my hips and onto the floor, exposing my thong and fleshy bottom. I stepped out of them but kept my boots on, now looking vulnerable and tough at the same time. He unfastened my bra, removing it to let my full breasts fall free, then started to take the pictures. I felt a strangely arousing sensation as my erect nipples traced patterns in the pasted surface as they were dragged across the sticky paper when I reached for the far edge, and, when I looked down at my glistening, smeared breasts, I felt them swell even more. I shakily folded the paper and climbed the stepladder before hanging it and cutting it to size. All the time he wandered around me, taking what seemed like dozens of photographs. I began to feel incredibly good, and I had a clear idea now what it was that turned him on, and I wasn't going to disappoint.

He watched me intently as I laid out another piece of paper ready for pasting, feeling unusually free and sexy as I leaned across the table. I got paste on me, of course, as he knew I would. He was focused on the view of my rear end, and I shimmied my arse for him as I worked, then, in a moment of unscripted imagination, I removed my pants, stood legs akimbo, still with my back to him, charged the brush, and brought it back between my legs, pasting myself from bum hole to cunt, the touch of the thousands of bristles teasing open my sex lips, paste splattering noisily on the floor as it fell from me in huge drips. I stifled a gasp of pleasure, but he could not deny his.

'Oh yes,' I heard him say excitedly. 'Oh yes, oh yes, oh yes!' I heard the camera one last time, and then suddenly he was right behind me, his cock out, and his hands on my nipples, cupping my breasts, kneading them in time to my sweeping brush strokes. His erection nuzzled between my sticky buttocks as he moved in close enough to press me against the table, then, without warning, he lifted me by the hips and spun me around to face him before sitting me squarely onto the pasting table, completely ignoring the fact that I was dropped onto the glistening upturned, expensive paper.

'Here, watch it,' I warned. 'That's about forty quid a roll, isn't it?'

He looked at me grinning with happiness and arousal. 'Who cares? It's me that's paying,' he said, his outstretched palms fighting for purchase on the slippery surface. Suddenly, and not to my surprise, there was an ominous crack and the flimsy table collapsed, folding in two so that we were both deposited in the 'v' as it landed on the floor, to be hit a split second later by the bowlful of paste as it slid towards us.

Needless to say I came off worst, as the entire pale-grey stickiness enveloped my midriff. There was suddenly complete silence until I began to giggle uncontrollably, and his concerned expression was replaced by one of unbridled amusement. He apologetically surveyed the state I was in.

'Sorry,' he said, faking a serious expression. 'I don't normally come so quickly, but it's been so very, very long.'

'Yeah right,' I said, smearing the paste around his stiff cock. I grasped it gently and clambered to my feet, before placing his eager hand between my legs. 'Fuck me or I'll report you to the Master Decorators' Guild.'

'No, not that!' he said, in mock horror. 'Anything but that! I'll do anything you say!' I knew he meant it.

'What are you waiting for?' I asked, as he hesitated momentarily. He knelt down and drew his fingernails tantalisingly along the inside of my thighs, then pushed me gently towards and into the shower room, where he cleaned me off before kneeling down and lifting one of my legs onto his shoulder. He began to lick me like a cat, long deliberate strokes up along my inner thighs, teasing my clitoris, darting back towards my anus as he lifted me higher, and I held onto him and shivered with delight as he tongued me.

'Are we on camera?' I asked, parting my legs as far as I could. He nodded guiltily. 'So this is my audition,' I purred, smiling.

'Ours,' he replied. The significance was not lost on me. I raised my eyes momentarily, motioned to him to let me go and knelt before him, taking his cock into my mouth. It was the first time that I spotted the little eye in the corner of the shower, filming everything.

He felt and tasted so good, so satisfying, and I licked and sucked, feeling his hips bucking in ecstasy as I worked on him. I caressed his balls and traced my index finger to the entrance to his anus, just pressing inside far enough to take him over the limit, and, at the last moment, as his glans jerked, I pulled his cock from my mouth and directed his spunk across my face and breasts, using my hands to spread it over me, its salty muskiness seeming to envelope us. He returned the compliment, his tongue renewing its interest on my clit until I orgasmed with an intensity that triggered my own shower onto him, his face and hair being marked with the scent of my release. I felt spent, satisfied, animal, and he was still beneath me, panting, when some thing occurred to me.

'Who took the photographs?' I asked.

'I did,' he said, simply.

I was perplexed. I had jumped to the wrong conclusion.

'Then who was . . .?'

'It was Simon, the new interior designer, Sally's boyfriend. Anyway, enough of them. I'm a bit of a voyeur, as you can probably tell. And those two are exhibitionists, of course! When I saw you in the paper, I thought to myself, 'She looks a game girl, a bit tough, just how I like 'em.'

I'd always gone for guys that were earthy and traditional; I'd never been out with a posh suit type before, but I would never judge by appearances again.

'So many girls don't want to get messy,' he said, 'but you don't mind and I love that. I think I may have found my kindred spirit.'

'So do I,' I said, as Josh helped me to my feet, his cock stiffening as he embraced me. 'And the customer is always right.'

I was about to become an apprentice again.

The Swimming Pool
Caroline Martin

The sudden lurch of the aircraft, accompanied by crackly instructions from the pilot to fasten our seatbelts until we were through the turbulence, jolted me from my sleep and back into panicked consciousness. I stared, stricken, out of the window and watched the wing dip into an endless sky. I closed my eyes and exhaled slowly and deliberately in an attempt to force my body into a state of serenity.

'You've missed dinner,' my friend Kate told me. 'It was a real treat too. Chicken in an unidentifiable sauce, soggy veg, a dry bread roll and a dollop of something masquerading as a crème brûlée.' She rolled her eyes and passed me a couple of miniatures and a plastic glass. 'Here. Thought you'd need a G and T to calm you down when you woke up.'

'Oh, you wonderful creature,' I gushed, unscrewing the bottles and pouring their contents into the glass.

'I have to say, you certainly seemed to be having nice dreams. You were smiling and kept giggling and towards the end you shouted out, "Oh, yes, like that, yes!" She thrashed her head from side to side, with an ecstatic look on her face.

'I did not!' I protested, trying not to laugh at her ridiculous display.

'Well, all right, not the last bit. But you were grinning from ear to ear and did have a couple of chuckles. Thinking of a certain gorgeous Scotsman by any chance?' She knocked back half her glass of gin and looked at me expectantly.

I smiled at the recollection of my recent encounter with a muscular, sandy-haired Scot. Less than 24 hours ago we had met – and then got rather well acquainted – at a party hosted by a mutual friend. I didn't know his name, exactly where he was from, how old he was or what he did for a living. Beyond his physicality I knew nothing about him, just as he knew nothing about me. And there was the thrill of it: locking eyes with a stranger, the silent agreement, urgent fumbling, the discovery of new flesh, new scent, the sensation of new hands exploring my body, loss of inhibitions. And afterwards, a kiss on the cheek, a shy 'goodbye', maybe even a 'thank you', my feverish body still humming and tingling. And then gone.

'It's going to get you in trouble one day,' Kate said, suddenly serious.

'What is?'

'Your penchant for shagging strangers.'

I giggled and took another slug of my G and T.

'I mean it,' she said. 'It could be really dangerous, you know.'

'He was a friend of George's and we were at George's house.' I tutted. 'What was going to happen?'

She sighed, exasperated. 'I'm not just talking

about last night, I'm talking generally. They could be anyone. One of them could turn out to be a right nutter.'

'You make it sound like there's been a few hundred,' I protested.

She arched a golden eyebrow.

'Hey, don't be mean.' I paused to sip my rapidly disappearing drink before venturing, 'Anyone would think you're jealous.'

It was her turn to laugh. 'Worried, yes. Curious even. Jealous, no, not at all. I've got my James.' She smiled dreamily.

'Well, as a happy singleton, I'm free to do as I please.' I frowned, suddenly concerned about my friend's attitude towards me. 'I don't sleep with just anyone, you know,' I said quietly.

She gave my arm a squeeze and smiled. 'I know you don't, darling. Just be careful though, that's all I'm saying.'

The plane wavered violently again, causing our bottles and glasses to slide across our pull-down tables. I failed to contain a strained squeak – it erupted from my mouth before I could stop it – and I gripped my armrests tightly until my knuckles faded to white.

'For God's sake . . .' Kate laughed and pushed the call button above our heads. A smiling air steward miraculously appeared. 'Two more G and Ts, please,' Kate said. Then, glancing at me she added, 'In fact, let's make those doubles.'

An hour and a half and several gins later, Kate and I tipsily dragged our suitcases from Chania airport and slung them into the baggage hold of our transfer coach. High-spirited but exhausted, we nodded off instantly and were awoken twenty minutes later when we arrived at our apartments. Within minutes we had checked in and collapsed into our beds.

For the next few days Kate and I hung out at the local beach. We drenched ourselves in oil and lay impatiently under the sun, enjoying the sensation of its fiery tongue licking every inch of our heat-starved bodies. We read trashy novels, listened to cheesy compilation CDs and studied our fellow beach-dwellers with a keen interest. Our nights were spent sipping margaritas and flirting with olive-skinned locals but Kate's words about my sexual habits were still at the forefront of my mind so, at the end of each evening, it was Kate's arm I looped my own through as I made my way home to bed.

On our fourth day, Kate's skin began to blister. I stroked cooling aloe vera over the irritation but it failed to soothe her chest and arms, which raged with prickly heat. She scratched her flesh in a savage effort to ease the persistent itching but her clawing simply exacerbated the condition.

'It's no good.' She sighed. 'I need to stay in the shade today.'

I frowned and stroked her hair. 'Well, let's hire a car and visit somewhere,' I suggested.

She shook her head. 'I've just had too much sun. I'd rather stay here. I'll put the air-con on and chill out with a book, then, hopefully, I'll be fine later. You go to the beach.'

I protested but Kate was insistent that her 'contamination' shouldn't spoil my holiday, so in the end we compromised and I agreed to sunbathe around our apartment's pool so that I could pop back and keep an eye on her. I stepped into my swimwear, tied a sarong around my waist and, after casting a concerned look at Kate, who waved more cheerfully than I'm sure she felt, headed out of our apartment.

The pool was busy and I was only just in time to secure one of the few remaining sun loungers. Once settled I opened my book and absorbed myself in the preposterous tale of a supermarket checkout girl who somehow met and married a rock god before becoming a Hollywood starlet in her own right. I wasn't quite sure what had possessed me to buy such a novel but it was easy reading and I found myself enjoying its escapist romanticism despite my cynical nature.

The heat was intense and beads of sweat began to form on my skin. I rested my book against my chest, pages splayed open, careful to avoid losing my place, and ran the back of my hand over my sizzling forehead.

A cold shower of water sprayed my legs and feet as someone jumped into the pool in front of me. My body jolted upright at the suddenness of the unexpected shower, unbalancing my book which slid from my body and slammed shut as it impacted with the ground. I frowned and turned to look in the direction of the pool.

And that was when I saw her.

A stunning golden-haired woman, perhaps 30

years old, grabbed a lilo, which floated beside her. Her toned tanned arms hoisted it from the water and flung it on to the concrete surrounding the edge of the pool. As she swam to the nearest edge I propped myself up on my elbows, rapt in the sight of her.

With effortless grace, she eased herself out of the pool and made her way to the shower. She gasped as icy crystals burst from the shower head, her body flinching and momentarily swerving away from the spray. She laughed lightly before diving under the water again, this time remaining under the powerful jet. Her nipples visibly hardened under the sodden clingy fabric of her swimsuit; they stood erect, poking through the cloth as though eager to escape the chilly water and seek solace once more in the sun. She raised her lithe arms to her head and smoothed her hair as the water gushed over her scalp and face and then cascaded over her shoulders. Her smooth bronze skin shone with the slick combination of water and sun lotion. She looked like a goddess.

My gaze followed her movements as she returned to her sunbed by the poolside. Dripping fat, liquid splodges on the ground, she snatched up her towel then hesitated. She did not wrap it around her as I thought she would but flung it on to her lounger, hooked her thumbs beneath her straps and peeled her swimsuit down. I held my breath as she lowered the fabric over her chest. Full, firm, lusciously round breasts bounced free from their confines. Her nipples which I had just witnessed stiffen under the shower, relaxed a little as they basked under the hot sun, but they were still the longest nipples I had ever seen. I imagined what it would be like to suck them, to feel them harden and extend into my mouth, to rub them with my fingertips, pinching and squeezing the juicy buds until they were rock. I felt my own nipples tighten inside my bikini top and became aware of a growing dampness between my legs.

'You must be careful.'

I jumped guiltily and then turned towards the direction of the voice. Janis, the barman, was collecting glasses. He came to stand in front of me, obscuring my view of the woman.

'You are very pink here.' He touched my cheek gently with the back of his hand. 'And here too,' he continued, grazing his fingertips across my collarbone. 'You are burning.'

Flustered, I shook my head. 'I'm OK.'

He frowned. 'You are very red. It is very hot under the sun at this time of day. It can be dangerous.' He bent down and reached to the side of my sunbed, from where he extracted an empty water bottle. I glanced over his broad tanned shoulder. The woman was now lying on her front, motionless except for an irregular tapping motion of her right foot as she joined the rhythm of whatever music was playing in her headphones.

I sighed.

'Sorry,' Janis said. 'You want me to leave the bottle here?'

'No, no, it's fine. Perhaps you're right. I'll sit in the shade for a little while.'

He nodded. 'Yes, you should cool down.'

I wandered to the shady bar area, closely followed by Janis carrying a precarious tower of glasses and empty bottles.

'Just another water, please.' I perched on a bar stool and placed a couple of coins on the bar.

'So,' he said, setting down my drink and scooping the money into the till, 'are you enjoying yourself here?'

I nodded as I sucked some liquid through a straw. 'Very much.'

'It is very beautiful here, yes? Lots of beautiful things to look at?'

I thought of the woman in the shower and fought the temptation to glance back at her now to see what she was doing. 'Oh, yes, the mountains are wonderful,' I said quickly, taking another sip of my water. 'And the sea's so clear.'

He grinned. 'But you don't need the beach when you can stay here.' He opened his arms in an expansive gesture, sweeping the pool and bar area. 'Everything you need is here, yes?'

I grinned back. 'It certainly is.'

Our conversation was interrupted by several heads bobbing over the edge of the bar.

'Can we have some ice cream?' a group of boys chorused.

Janis smiled and guided the children to the freezer at the other end of the bar. 'Now, what you would like?'

I turned towards the blonde woman who was still lying on her front and sighed again as I remembered the way she had looked as she had emerged from the water; the way her body had responded so brazenly to the changes in temperature as she flung herself into the icy shower and then dried herself under the sun. The way I had felt such a powerful desire as I watched her.

My thoughts were broken by the presence of a man who, despite an empty bar area, came and stood right beside me, so close that his thigh nudged mine as he stood waiting to catch Janis's eye. I had watched him dive into the pool earlier. Or, rather, I had looked up from my summer reading just in time to see his tight buttocks encased in skimpy black Speedos. I could see now that the sight of him from the front was even more breathtaking. His trunks clung unapologetically to his crotch. The size and fullness of his balls were clearly visible; they hung heavily, barely contained, it seemed, by the fabric of the trunks which stretched to contain their weight. His cock too was on display, its length and form showcased by the flimsy damp material. I stared at its bulging crudeness; it looked obscene. Many women, I imagine, would have looked away disgusted but I felt an aching need between my legs and shifted uncomfortably on my stool.

Janis returned and signalled that he had run out of cold beers. He hurriedly offered to fetch more from the storeroom and the man nodded appreciatively and leaned forwards, resting his hands on the bar. He was bulky; tall and broad with a thick neck and square jaw. His dark hair was cut short although the presence of stubble suggested that he had not shaved for two or three days. All in all, he was attractive, although his facial features and general physique failed to hold my attention for very long. After a preliminary scan my eyes were drawn once more to his bulging Lycra-clad package.

I just had to touch that cock.

Without pausing for a moment to consider what I was doing, I shifted to the edge of my stool and reached out my hand. I placed my open palm flat to the front of his Speedos and pressed gently but firmly. His body instantly jolted upright and he turned to look at me, parting his lips slightly as though to speak. For a moment I was anxious, concerned that he was about to reject my attention, but I left my hand hovering in front of his crotch and he quickly closed his mouth again. I stood up and, without speaking, eased into a position which would conceal my action without alerting suspicion. I pressed him again, harder this time. He groaned softly and closed his eyes as I began to rub in circular motions across the front of his crotch. I increased my rhythm, feeling his bulge swell until I could not stand it any longer. I gripped his shaft through the fabric and squeezed along his length. With my other hand I cupped his balls, alternating soft caresses with firm squeezes. The head now poked over the top of his trunks, a shimmering wet bead visible on the tip. I peered over his shoulder and scanned the pool area; no one was looking in our direction and we remained alone at the bar.

I pushed the front of his trunks down, releasing his straining cock which eagerly sprang free. His eyes flew open in alarm and he took a step back.

'It's OK, no one's looking.' My voice sounded husky, urgent. I couldn't bear the possibility that this would be the end of our encounter.

I looked down at the muscled column of flesh. Now fully erect it lay stretched and taut against his belly. I reached for the tip, circling the tiny slit with my thumb, smearing his juices over and around the head. He closed his eyes again and clenched his jaw. Enveloping the length of him, I slid my hand up and down his hardness, squeezing him and twisting my wrist a little as I gripped him tightly. I peered over his shoulder once more, amazed that no one had noticed our activity. My gaze settled again on the blonde woman from the shower who was shifting position. I gasped as she sat upright, exposing those delicious raspberry-pink nipples once more. Then I gasped again as my bikini knickers were yanked aside and a determined finger dipped straight into my wetness. I tugged his cock more forcefully, pumping him hard as he rubbed my clitoris and pushed one then two fingers inside me.

All the time, I watched the woman who had begun to apply sun cream to her front. I could smell my own arousal as I watched her massage the lotion into her breasts, paying particular attention to her sensitive buds. The cock in my hand began to twitch and I could feel the tension in the man's thighs and arse as he tried to resist the urge to thrust. I squeezed his full balls with my left hand while the right pulled at him roughly. His breath ripped out of him in short sharp bursts. As his fingers found my swollen nub again, I closed my eyes and imagined that his finger was her erect nipple, rubbing and agitating my wet clit and sliding inside me.

Within seconds, I felt a sudden hot heady rush as a powerful orgasm surged through my body. While my pelvic muscles contracted violently with each wave of pleasure, I strained against my body's natural instinct to jerk and buck. Flinging my hips back I slammed my buttocks into the bar, accidentally releasing my grip on the man. His expression was pained but before I had time to grasp it again he had grabbed himself with the same fingers that were slick with my juices. It was the most exquisite sight.

'That's right,' I murmured as he tightened his grip on himself, 'I want to see you work your cock.'

'Oh, fuck.' His eyes were shut tight and he moaned as he began to stroke himself. Despite the previous frenzied activity when my hand had been wrapped around his shaft, pumping him until he looked ready to burst, he began tentatively with long, steady strokes.

'Do it faster,' I quietly ordered him.

He grunted and increased his strokes.

'Yes,' I breathed, 'do it really hard.'

With both hands on himself, rubbing and pulling, he began in earnest to fuck his own hand.

Unbelievably aroused, I reached for his balls, which were pulled up high and tight, desperate for release, cupping and squeezing them. At once I felt his entire body stiffen.

'Fuck,' he growled. 'Oh, God, I'm going to . . .'

Leaning forwards slightly he gripped the edge of

the bar with one hand and grimaced as his cock went into spasm.

We both stood wordlessly for a few seconds, hot and breathless. He rearranged his Speedos and I checked myself to ensure my own modesty, although it was probably too late to be worrying about that. The man and I both looked up at the same time and met each other's gaze. He smiled, awkwardly at first and then rather arrogantly.

A dark-haired woman approached us and jabbed him in the shoulder. 'What have you been doing all this time?'

He shrugged and mumbled something.

She sighed overdramatically and reached between us, picking up a couple of bottles from the bar. 'It's a wonder our beers aren't warm now,' she complained. 'They've been sitting on here for five minutes and that's all it takes in this heat.'

Five minutes?

The man and I looked up immediately, scanning the bar for Janis who was nowhere in sight.

'Men!' She tutted, grinning at me. 'What can you do with them?' Bottles of beer in hand, she nudged the man's arm and steered him back to their sun loungers.

When I returned to our apartment shortly afterwards, Kate was sitting on her bed watching a Greek soap opera.

'This is great,' she said without looking up. 'The man with the moustache is married to the blonde who's pregnant with the other man with the moustache's baby. And her dad's just left her mum for another woman who, unbeknown to him, has just been killed in a tragic moped accident. And I got all that without subtitles.' She shook her head in wonderment. 'Amazing.'

I laughed. 'You don't look so red now. Still itchy?'

She shrugged. 'A bit.'

I stood at the foot of her bed. 'It's boiling today,' I said, somewhat redundantly.

Kate smiled and nodded. She looked at the book in my hand and pointed to my bookmark. 'You didn't get very far. Too busy to read?'

'What do you mean?' I carried my damp towel on to the balcony where I concentrated on draping it across the area with far more precision than was necessary.

'Well . . .' Kate stood behind me, hands on hips. 'There's always so much to do around the pool, isn't there?' she said sweetly. 'So many new people to meet.' She stretched luxuriously and smiled, then leaned forwards and rested on the balcony wall. 'You know, it was so nice out here at lunchtime.'

'I thought you were staying in all day? Why didn't you come down to the pool?'

She shook her head. 'It was shady up here then; lovely and cool. Not nearly as hot as down there. It looked positively scorching from where I was sitting.' She grinned mischievously and tilted her head slightly, a signal for me to take in the view.

I went to stand beside her and stared speechless at the sight before me.

'The pool, the bar . . . what a fantastic vantage point we have from here,' she said. 'I didn't know we overlooked all that, did you?'

'No.' My voice caught in my throat as I continued to stare at the bar area.

'Tell you what,' she said brightly, 'I'll get us some wine from the fridge and then you can tell me all about it.'

Kate and I talked into the early hours and drank three bottles of wine between us before we finally drifted into sleep. She quizzed me about Speedo-man, demanding every last detail. But although she was fascinated and shrieked with delight at my lurid confessions, I couldn't help but remember her disapproving words of a few days before. She, like my other friends, teased me about my sexual voracity and expressed concerns, yet was also keen to hear about my encounters. They seemed to take a vicarious pleasure in my sinful tales, as though it made their own safe lives in their safe relationships suddenly wild and exotic. I took their jibes with good humour but wished they could accept my choices without fuss. So, I refused to be brainwashed into searching for my Mr Darcy. So what? What was I missing out on? Monotonous weekends of takeaways, *Football Focus* and the missionary position?

I wanted passion. When I felt a body against mine, I wanted to feel raw emotion − ragged lust and the purest desire. I wanted to take and be taken and be shaken to my very core. I wanted to lose every inch of my being in that moment; to feel so in tune with my body, my mind and my lover that the experience was almost spiritual; to feel sensual explosions that take days to recover from.

All women want this, don't they? The only difference between my friends and me is that, unlike me, they don't believe they can actually have it.

I woke up just after nine feeling distinctly hungover and dragged my dehydrated body into the shower. Feeling ravenous I hunted in the kitchen cupboards only to find nothing remotely palatable. Kate was still softly snoring so I wrapped my sarong around my hips, pulled on a vest and stepped into my sandals, then made my way out of the apartment complex and on to the narrow road beyond. I had heard our next door neighbours talking on their balcony about a wonderful bakery a few minutes walk away, so I decided to set off to find it and bring back some brunch for Kate and me.

A few minutes walk away became half an hour of my being lost. As I continued to turn down winding streets lined with tiny white houses I desperately tried to get my bearings, but it was hopeless. I had underestimated how hot it would be and had not worn a hat – my head throbbed in the heat and I could feel the back of my neck burning as half an hour stretched into an hour.

Just as I felt ready to drop to my knees and weep, I spotted a man coming out of one of the houses.

'Um ... *kalimera*.' My voice was weak. 'I'm, um, looking for the ... erm ... the bakery,' I said, waving my hands wildly in the hope that my gesticulating would somehow indicate bread. 'The, um, *boulangerie*?' I said feebly.

He smiled and said in perfect English, 'Just around the corner.'

I thanked him profusely before stumbling around the bend, feeling dizzy and slightly sick. Within seconds I was standing in front of the pastry Mecca I had set out to find almost two hours before. And then I fainted.

'Are you OK?' The voice was soothing and full of concern.

I tried to focus and my vision gradually became sharper. Staring down at me – a vision of compassionate concern – was the woman from the swimming pool.

I struggled to sit up and she handed me a glass of water. Beside her stood an elderly man wearing a white apron – the baker, I presumed – who looked just as anxious.

'Sorry,' I mumbled between thirsty gulps of water. 'How long was I out for?'

The woman looked at her watch. 'Oh, er –' she looked thoughtful '– about four seconds,' she said, smiling.

I laughed and the man gently helped me to my feet. The coolness of the shop and the water had made me feel considerably better already.

'I think you're staying at the same apartments as me,' the woman said.

'That's right,' I said without hesitation. I felt myself blush slightly and added, 'I think I saw you by the pool yesterday.'

She smiled and nodded. 'Well, what about if I escort you back, just in case you pass out again?' She lifted up a couple of bags. 'I've bought plenty and I'm prepared to share.'

We walked at an easy pace, pausing every few

minutes so that she could check that I was OK. We chatted comfortably with each other about what we did back home and what we thought about the island. She was on holiday alone after her partner split up with her three days before the flight.

'Well, he sounds pretty stupid to me,' I said as our apartments came into sight.

She giggled. 'Thanks for the support. Actually though, he's a she.'

I felt my cheeks burn but a fluttering in my belly suggested that embarrassment was not the only emotion I felt.

We arrived at the block of apartments that adjoined Kate's and mine.

'Well, we're here but it looks like the maid is too,' she said, pointing to a trolley full of towels and toilet rolls outside her door. She smiled apologetically. 'I don't think I'll be such a great hostess with someone cleaning around our feet.'

I tried hard to conceal my disappointment. 'It doesn't matter.' I shrugged.

She looked thoughtful. 'Well, there's plenty here for your friend too. We could go to yours and just all share it out?'

'Fine,' I said, making every effort to sound nonchalant, and we set off for my apartment.

The apartment was empty when we entered. I picked up a scrawled note that Kate had left on my bed.

'Rash better. Gone to pool,' I read aloud.

We stood for a moment, suddenly awkward. The conversation that had flowed so freely earlier now deserted us.

'I could go back?' she said at last.

'No,' I blurted.

She raised an eyebrow flirtatiously and I felt my stomach dip and twirl.

'Well,' I said hastily, 'if you want to ...'

'If I want to what?' She smiled mischievously, enjoying my obvious discomfort.

'If you want to go back, then you should go back,' I babbled, 'although if you wanted to stay, then obviously ...'

Before I had a chance to register, she took hold of my hand. Excitement and fear were a toxic concoction and I struggled to catch my breath as she pressed her lips against mine. I marvelled at their warm softness. As she pushed harder against me I cradled the back of her head, weaving my fingers into her silky hair. She grazed her teeth across my lips, catching my bottom lip, and I moaned as she gently tugged at my tingling flesh. Her tongue eased my lips apart and I sucked on it, pulling her deeper into my mouth. She moved her head away and looked directly into my eyes, stroking my left cheek with the gentlest caress I had ever experienced. The sensation made my skin prickle and I was overwhelmed by the way it aroused my whole body – with the slightest touch this beautiful woman had ignited my entire being. Her green eyes shone as I mirrored her actions, stroking her with what I hoped was a touch as delicate and sensual as hers. She closed her eyes and leaned into me, sighing against my ear.

'You smell lovely,' she whispered, nudging against my neck.

Excitement gripped my chest and I seized her head and pushed her closer to my hot skin. She licked and sucked and nibbled at my taut flesh and I gasped and moaned in shocked delight at the agonising pleasure her actions caused. She increased the pressure of her tongue, sliding it wetly down my neck and along my collarbone, expertly stimulating erogenous zones I didn't know I had. Despite the fact that they had not been touched, my nipples swelled and tightened, standing erect and pushing almost painfully against my skimpy vest top. I bit my bottom lip in an attempt to stifle my moans.

Still with the lightest touch, she slid her fingers beneath my straps and pulled them agonisingly slowly down my arms. I held my breath as she revealed my breasts and felt my legs weaken as she licked each of my nipples in turn, teasing them into ever-stiffer peaks. I watched her lapping at my breasts, amazed by the response she was creating in me. She closed her lips around one of my hard nipples, sucking hungrily.

I tentatively reached for her, curious to touch her body and see how she responded. I carefully lifted her T-shirt until it rested high on her chest. I took in the sight of her bare breasts and murmured my approval before tenderly cupping each one. While she continued to lick and tease my nipples, I squeezed her gently, enjoying the fullness in my hands. I had never touched another woman in this way and the beauty of her body, the sensual passion of the encounter and the wetness that seeped into my knickers thrilled me.

I grazed her prominent nipples with the tips of my thumbs, enjoying their rough texture and was surprised and delighted by how much larger they became at my touch, how they stiffened and puckered as I rubbed and teased them. Curiosity and arousal got the better of me, defeating any concerns I may have had about not knowing how to please a woman, and I caught each long nipple between forefingers and thumbs and rubbed them harder. I felt unbearably aroused by the sight and sensation of feeling them under my skin, while she continued to work my own into a lustful frenzy. As I pulled them hard, she cried out and bit one of my nipples with such force that I arched my back and experienced a light-headed sensation, immediately followed by a molten spasm in my crotch.

I was amazed by my body's intense response and welcomed her mouth as she moved to kiss me again and pressed her body closely to mine. Although satisfied by my unexpected climax, I wanted more than ever to touch her. As we kissed, I let my hands skim down her back – I desperately wanted her to experience the pleasures I had just felt.

A loud knocking at the door startled us and we leaped apart like guilty teenagers.

'Erm, it sounds like you're quite busy...' It was Kate's voice. 'But I've forgotten my key and I really need to come in. So, if you and the lucky man could just make yourselves respectable...'

The woman and I collapsed into giggles and rearranged our clothing.

'I can hide on the balcony?' she whispered.

I laughed. 'No need. It'll be worth it to see the look on her face.'

I opened the door and Kate raced in.

'I'm so desperate for the loo,' she wailed, pushing past me and heading to the bathroom.

'Why didn't you use the one by the pool?' I asked.

'Roaches.'

When she emerged, she noticed the woman standing in the kitchen for the first time. She raised her eyebrows in surprise, then forced her features into a casual expression. 'Hi,' she said warmly.

'Hi – and bye,' said the woman. 'I'm just leaving.' She signalled to the carrier bags and then looked at me and winked. 'Enjoy the buns.'

Grinning, I walked to the door with her.

'Perhaps I'll see you later?' she said.

I nodded and waved as she walked towards her apartment. Closing the door, I smiled at the surreal situation.

'You might well smile!' Kate bellowed. 'Oh my God!'

'It's not a big deal,' I said, blushing.

Kate looked wide-eyed and headed towards the fridge. 'I think,' she said, taking out a bottle of wine, 'you and I need to have a little chat.'

Customer Satisfaction
Maya Hess

It wasn't that Adele Riley enjoyed shopping as such. It wasn't that she wore or understood or even drove her most frivolous purchases. Her wardrobes bulged, her house was filled with the latest technology and her driveway boasted several classic cars as well as a jet ski, a motor home and a small yacht that she'd recently just had to have.

No, it was the handing over of the cash that drove Adele wild – and she always shopped with cash – the easy deal between herself and a hungry salesman; the flicker beneath his glinting eyes as they were briefly connected by a wad of notes; the hardening of his jaw, his forearms, his expression, as he counted out the money several times. It was the potential and the power contained within those little bits of printed paper that thrilled Adele most. The impending burst of authority it gave her. Plus, it also showed that she was loaded.

But once the deal was done and the goods were delivered, once the packaging had been ripped off and the items were no longer pristine, when the thrill of the hunt was over and the open sign switched to closed, Adele pined for yet another frivolous purchase. It was the rush of guilt combined with adrenalin combined with sheer decadence that she was doing something reckless considering that, even though she pretended to be rich, she wasn't really at all.

The phone call came just as the Mercedes salesman came deep inside her. Adele fumbled with her Nokia as she was shunted against the wall, her skirt hitched up over her thighs and one stocking wilting at her ankle.

'Yes?' she snapped. The gathering pulses in her sex joined together in what she knew would be an unstoppable orgasm. She really didn't want to be talking on the phone. But as she listened to what the caller had to say, Adele slowly slid down the wall, pulling her newest lover down to the floor with her as her mouth dropped open and her eyes grew wide and as black as beach pebbles.

Mercedes Man, puzzled, withdrew from his prospective client and took the opportunity to lever his long wet erection between her plump although shocked lips. If this didn't work, he thought, he would sink his face between Adele's tanned thighs. He adored beautiful women; all women. Especially ones who were ripe for a forty thousand pound deal.

'That's disgusting!' she exclaimed, as the stretched wet tip of the erection bumped her lips. 'I just won't allow it!' Adele snapped her phone shut and clamped her mouth around the super-sized treat, relieving the salesman of his concern that she had been referring to his cock. 'Mmm,' she mumbled, gripping the base and taking him deep, getting right back to what she did best: sex and shopping.

The ten per cent deposit was handed over on a less than usual high. The fuck had been good. Not the best ever but enough to get her wet all over again as she gave up, note by note, four thousand delicious pounds. Adele noticed that Mercedes Man – Mr Coombes, Senior Sales Executive – had grown hard again beneath the cut of his fine wool suit. At least there was the balance still to pay. Adele's eyes narrowed to slits as she imagined handing over thirty-six grand but then she grew angry at the thought of the phone call.

'If you could kindly pay the balance by next Thursday, I'll make sure that your new vehicle is sparkling and ready for you, Miss Riley.' Mr Coombes allowed himself an unprofessional visual slurp of his client's breasts. He couldn't help it. Her blouse was sheer, she was braless, her nipples were freshly sucked and, by the look of them, eager for more. He couldn't wait for Miss Riley to pick up her car.

'Next Thursday?' Adele asked. 'That's not much over a week. I'll be paying cash you know.' Her voice was clipped and betrayed nothing of their recent liaison in the photocopying room.

'Is there a problem?' Mr Coombes ran a finger around his collar. He didn't want to lose his commission and certainly didn't want to jeopardise another chance to fuck the divine woman sitting in front of him. He'd meant to have her from behind but had come too soon. Next time, he promised himself, wishing that Mrs Coombes would occasionally oblige.

'Of course there isn't a problem,' Adele snapped.

She gathered up the paperwork and stuffed it in her Prada bag. 'Thursday next it is then,' she promised, forcing a smile. She knew, as things now stood with her bank manager, it would be impossible.

The cash machine devoured five of her eight debit and credit cards and the bank cashier refused Adele to even withdraw ten pounds for a ride home.

'Does madam not have a car to go home in? I see that you have five car loans in your name.' The young woman offered a safe leer behind the security glass.

'Of course I have a car. Several, in fact.' Adele swallowed the knot gathering in her throat. She hesitated and retrieved her cheque book and remaining cards from the chute. 'They are all being serviced and polished today.' This was the hardest thing she had ever had to do. 'Could I possibly withdraw five pounds then?' Truth was, Adele couldn't stand paying the extortionate city centre parking fees while on her shopping sprees and preferred to save cash by taking the bus. There was no thrill in feeding a car-park machine when all you got in return was a ticket. A girl had to be careful with her money.

'No, sorry. Like I said, your account is frozen. I suggest you contact your branch manager.'

'Oh I will!' Adele snapped, realising that she was truly penniless. 'How about a pound then?' she asked, offering her most alluring expression.

Dinner was crackers and jam because she had no food in the house and had exactly 27 pence in her purse. Normally on a Friday night, Adele would treat herself and several friends to dinner at an expensive restaurant. She'd promised everyone a feast at the new Thai place but had to feign sickness instead of suffering the embarrassment of having her credit card declined even though it was her finances that were ill, not Adele.

'Shame,' Nick commiserated. 'We'll miss you, Addie, but you get yourself better real soon now.'

'I will,' Adele mumbled down the phone through several tissues to make herself sound unwell. She knew what he really meant was that they would miss her paying the bill although any one of her high-earning friends − Nick the IT consultant included − could afford to pay. It was just that Adele *liked* to pay. She insisted. Always. It was a power thing: unlocking the potential of the cash, however much it was costing her in interest.

To pass the time and until a plan formed (crazy things occurred to her such as seducing her bank manager or, ridiculously, selling off her assets) Adele spent the evening on the internet browsing the most exclusive online boutiques, piling her virtual shopping cart high with goods before making a speedy exit at the last possible moment when her credit card details were required. The pretend cyber-shopping spree didn't even come close to the thrill of buying in the flesh.

'Buying in the flesh,' she whispered to herself, thinking, wondering, plotting. She poured herself another glass of water, pretending it was Rioja. 'Buying flesh, more like,' she said with a giggle while simultaneously Googling the words. Nothing much came up, sadly, because she fancied a bit of sexy diversion from her money worries. There were plenty of dating sites and chat rooms, she knew, but what she really needed was something that combined the buzz of shopping with the naughtiness of seducing the salesman, which she invariably did.

By late evening, Adele had grown desperate and miserable. She'd been unable to find solace on the internet and she was still as broke as ever. 'God, send me a sign,' she said with a sigh, laying her head down on the desk. 'What am I going to do?'

For the first time since her bank manager had called earlier that morning, Adele realised the seriousness of her financial problems. She'd always thought of herself as well off, rich even. Her job as PA paid enough to secure a multitude of loans and credit cards but evidently not well enough to actually repay them. Really, securing cash whenever the whim took her hadn't ever been a problem. And she'd never once considered the prospect of paying it back.

Adele raised her head off the desk just as the email pinged her inbox. She was ready for bed, ready for a little self-comforting with her vibrator but the email, marked as spam, intrigued her.

Debt, Mortgage, Loans getting you down?
UNDERpaid and OVERspending?
Turn your unwanted items into cash – FAST!
Sell those frivolous purchases on our new
STRAPPED FOR CASH auction.
Special introductory offer . . .

'I'd have to sell *myself* to pay off my huge debts,' Adele said with a laugh, about to delete the email. But instead, she stopped and thought. 'Now there's an idea,' she mused, allowing her fingers to brush over the thin fabric of her blouse. Her nipples didn't need any encouraging; they were willing. 'I guess that's illegal,' she said with a sigh, wishing there was a way that she could advertise herself for a date, charge a fortune for the privilege and then, well, who knows.

The computer wheezed as she shut it down, her mind buzzing with possibilities. Just the thought of promoting her assets online drove Adele to strip in front of the mirror and size up what she had to offer. As an afterthought, she snapped the curtains shut. She had been known to play around with them wide open and the light on but now that she was considering selling herself for cash, then anyone who wanted a look would have to pay for it.

'Nothing's for free,' she told her reflection as she drew a line from her full breasts down to the neat V at the top of her exotic holiday-tanned legs. 'And that includes me,' she said with a giggle before dipping a finger between the delicate folds that fastened her most saleable product into a highly desirable package, as the man at the car showroom had found out earlier. For free.

'Just imagine how rich I'd be if they'd all paid for the pleasure of my body.' Then Adele folded herself onto the expensive bedding of her king-size bed and tried to place a value on her assets by climaxing over and over and doing despicable things with the vibrator that surely any man would pay to at least watch, if not join in. 'Forget shopping,' she said, exhausted. 'I'm going into sales and I –' she told herself naughtily, '– am the merchandise.'

It was an ingenious idea – one that would satisfy her craving for a deal and her appetite for men. Adele wondered why she hadn't thought of it before. Just how she would set about her new business venture and market herself, she wasn't entirely sure. She decided to sleep on the problem and dreamed of all her debts dissolving and as many men as she could possibly handle exchanging wads of cash for her insatiable body.

Monday morning and the office was teeming with impatient managers, sales executives guzzling coffee while pinning the phone to their ears, and the hum of business as usual as the staff settled into another week.

Adele, dressed in a designer suit that she had purchased before her financial ice age, slipped quietly into her office, shut the door and booted up her terminal. By the end of the morning, she wanted her new online shopping experience to be available to every man in the country. Her business mantra was simple: make love, make money.

The first time her mobile rang, she ignored it. She was deep in thought about getting herself exposed, literally, and didn't want distractions. But when it rang and rang insistently, Adele finally answered and was once again greeted by a less than patient bank manager.

'Plans are in hand, Mr Wetherby,' she purred

down the phone, 'to clear my debts within a matter of months.'

'Oh?' The manager sounded incredulous. And dull, thought Adele, imagining him in an unremarkable grey suit with matching hair and skin that had never seen a tropical beach or been adored by a passionate woman.

'Yes. Fear not, Adele Riley is going into business.' And, failing to impress Mr Wetherby one bit, he demanded that Adele liquidate her assets immediately.

'That's the plan exactly, Mr Wetherby. I can assure you that very very soon my best assets will be melting and earning me oodles of money.' Adele giggled and hung up. 'Right, back to work,' she said with a sigh and began trawling the internet for the type of website that she needed.

By lunch time, she was desperate. It seemed that no such site existed. Instead of her usual visit to the trendy wine bar for lunch, Adele walked several blocks through the city to Nick's glass and chrome office building. She found him eating a sandwich, bent over his laptop.

'Better now?' he asked without looking up.

'Fine,' Adele said, forgetting she'd been ill. 'Nick, I need you to build me a website. An auction website. By the end of today.' Adele offered her sweetest smile and widened her dark eyes. 'Pretty please?'

Nick pushed back in his chair and laughed. 'Addie, if you knew my schedule then you'd realise –'

'Even if I show you this?' Adele lifted her skirt to

reveal long slim legs gift wrapped in the sheerest stockings ever and topped off with a tiny strappy triangle of silk.

Nick swallowed, his chest rising from an involuntary breath in. 'No, not even if you show me that.' He returned to his work but was unable to even touch a key because Adele had thrust her hips towards his face.

'You can lick it,' she pleaded. 'And, if you get the work done today, you can have a three-hour fuck in lieu of payment.' She made sure that Nick caught a waft of her natural perfume by running her finger around the lace edge of her panties.

'Just how do you expect me to put that on my tax return?' His eyes narrowed and his lips parted a little at Adele's proximity. He'd always had a thing for her, like all the men in their circle of friends – she was gorgeous, stunning – but really, could he accept her body as payment?

'It's a deadline thing, Addie. A big banking client's expecting a presentation later and –'

Adele didn't want to hear excuses. She was a businesswoman now and had her own deadlines to meet. She lowered her thong and pulled Nick by his unruly blond hair, pressing his mouth into the cleft of her shaven pussy. He soon got the hang of it and purred resignedly as his tongue searched the neat little folds of his friend's most secret place.

'Oh, Nick,' Adele moaned. 'If your web design skills are half as brilliant as your tongue, then I'm going to make a fortune.'

'I can have it done by six,' Nick murmured, prising apart the sweet lips with his thumbs and driving his tongue deep inside. Then he stopped, looked up along Adele's flat tanned stomach and stared directly into her eyes. 'What, exactly, will you be selling?'

'Take a wild guess,' she said, giggling, and levered his mouth between her legs once again.

Back at her office, Adele cadged a sandwich off the receptionist but it didn't go halfway to satisfying her appetite. How she had finally pulled Nick from between her legs she didn't know, but leaving him without a string of orgasms had set her up for a difficult afternoon. What she had left his office with though was the promise that her new website would be up and running by early evening and all she had to do was list herself for sale by uploading some naughty photos and dirty promises.

After his initial shock at his friend's new venture, Nick had explained how they had an 'off-the-shelf' software product that would suit her needs completely and he would simply customise it to her desired look.

'Classy and expensive,' Adele had instructed. 'I'm going to be charging a fortune so keep it all upmarket.'

'No problemo,' Nick assured and set to work with an uncomfortable bulge in his trousers and three hours with Adele to look forward to later.

Back home from work, Adele couldn't eat even if she'd had food in the fridge. She kept visiting her new online home – a domain that Nick had kindly donated from their corporate stock with a suitably kinky name – but it wasn't until just before seven that Nick called round with the news that the site was finally live. He looked exhausted.

'It's fantastic!' Adele squealed as the page resolved. 'Just what I wanted.'

'I've got a couple of my guys to work overtime to promote it everywhere. They've done hundreds of adult sites so they know exactly where to get you noticed.' Adele lunged at him gratefully. 'That was an extra favour,' he said with a yawn. 'But one that should get your business up and running in no time.'

'Now for your payment.' Adele giggled, took Nick by the hand and guided him to her bedroom. But Nick glanced at his watch. 'Somewhere you'd rather be?' she asked.

'Of course not, except that I still have to see the banking client I mentioned earlier.'

'Poor Nicky,' Adele crooned, her voice enveloping his tired body like a bubble bath. She unbuttoned his shirt. 'Will you take some naughty photos of me for my website before you go? I need something to tease the punters with.'

Adele had already set up her professional quality, extremely expensive, bought-on-credit camera. The huge lens glared at the perfectly made bed and Nick stood behind it, studying the various settings.

'It suits you,' Adele said as she came into view on the camera's display. She had stripped naked and her smooth flesh and perfect breasts and flared hips and glossy long dark hair looked a million dollars on screen.

'What does?' Nick swallowed, pretending to adjust the camera. He zoomed in on her breasts, focusing on a nipple. He took a shot.

'Being behind the camera.' Adele climbed onto the bed, making sure that her legs were slightly apart as her buttocks passed in front of the lens. She heard a frenzy of clicking as Nick got to work.

Within an hour, Adele had a fine gallery of pictures to add to her website. Nick had left reluctantly but not before giving her a tutorial on how to get the best from her new auction site. Soon, a dozen tantalising auctions were on air, each advertising various dates, experiences and thrills and all accompanied by an array of sexy, alluring pictures to encourage opening bids.

The lowest starting price for an evening with Adele, including talking dirty, a sexy outfit and half an hour watching her play with a vibrator, was fifteen hundred pounds. She hoped to net double that. At the other end of the scale, Adele had implied total mind and body possession for twenty-four hours – a do-with-me-what-you-will auction – and the first offer over ten thousand pounds would secure the deal.

'Well, I only want rich people buying me,' Adele said with a grin as she viewed her lovely website. 'Mr Wetherby would be proud of me. I shall have my debts paid off in no time and all the fun a girl could want.'

There was no way Adele could sleep, especially as her body was aroused to the max because Nick had left before his promised payment. So she whiled away the hours by visiting chat rooms and discussion forums, especially the ones where she reckoned rich guys would hang out, and promoted her new website blatantly. Within several hours, she could see that hundreds had already visited her site.

And then it came. At ten thirty, Adele received a system email stating that someone had bid. The thrill! A stranger wanted to pay cash, so far a minimum of four thousand pounds, for the pleasure of her company and as much sex that could be crammed into three hours in a hotel. Adele's exclusive boutique was in business and, best of all, she was the merchandise. She could barely believe it was working. Mr Wetherby would eat his own financial words. *'Hopeless with money ... A shopaholic ... A liability to the bank...'* His insults had rained thick and fast.

As quickly as her fingers would allow, Adele took a look at the bidder's details but it was pointless because in another few minutes he had been out-bid by two hundred pounds and within an hour, nearly a hundred men had registered along with several women, and a dozen bids had been placed.

'This is amazing,' she mouthed as she watched her shopping debts melt away in front of her eyes. By morning, she would be able to call her bank manager and declare herself on the way to solvency again.

'I'm sorry but Mr Wetherby's phoned in sick today, Miss Riley. Can I take a message?' The woman was impatient, her tone clipped.

'Sure. Tell the miserable man that Miss Shopaholic called and she'll be depositing a large sum into her account very soon.' That should keep the weasel off my back, Adele thought, hanging up before the secretary could defend her boss.

Then she went to prepare herself for the biggest date of her life because – and it made her skin dance at the thought – a moment after midnight, someone had bid on The Big One. A stranger had agreed to pay ten thousand pounds to own Adele for twenty-four hours and really, at that price, she wanted to ensure he got the fuck of his life.

'This guy must like shopping, too,' she pondered as she stepped into a gossamer Versace dress, the fabric of which wrapped flimsily around the curves of her body. 'I do hope he pays in cash.' She felt the thin strand of satin between her legs dampen at the thought.

Adele strode confidently into the hotel lobby and was immediately faced with a hundred possibilities. Some kind of conference had attracted virtually every good-looking man in the country and picking out the mystery bidder from among the gathering of suited males would be tricky. Especially as she had no idea what he looked like. Suddenly, the worst occurred to Adele. What if he was ugly, dirty, a madman . . .

'I'd recognise you better without your clothes.' A hand was on her shoulder and a voice as reassuring as warm honey drizzled in her ear. She smelled expensive cologne, too. Adele turned.

'Oh,' she garbled. 'Are you . . . I mean, did you . . .'

'David,' he said, extending a hand. 'You are even more stunning in real life.'

'Oh,' Adele said again and found herself being led towards the lift. 'Are you, you know, the one who . . .' He could be anyone, after all.

'Cash OK with you?' He winked, raising a brown leather briefcase. Adele relaxed a little, knowing she was well on the way to getting the dreadful Mr Wetherby off her back.

'Fine,' she replied, feeling as if she'd downed three gin and tonics at once. The lift carried them to the fifth floor, by which time her vision was blurred and every nerve in her body stripped to the core. 'Absolutely fine.' And she nearly melted into the plush carpet as she watched David unlock the door to a magnificent suite.

The man was a god. If she'd hand-picked him herself, she couldn't have done better. He was tall, dressed perfectly in jeans that showed off the power of his legs and buttocks, and a pale shirt and linen jacket with his hair, ever so slightly greying in a way that told of experience not age, brushing the collar. He turned, his face essentially clean shaven but with a day's growth adding a rough edge to his impeccably smooth appearance, and said, 'After you.'

'Do you often buy your women on the internet?' Adele asked, quickly checking her appearance in the mirror. She had to think of repeat business.

'Impulse purchase.' He smiled, removing his jacket and laying it over a chair. He placed the briefcase on the king-size bed and clicked it open. Adele begged her mouth not to drop open as a diamond-like radiance burst from within the case. 'Would you like to count it?'

'Oh, yes please.' Adele's fingers twitched at the chance to touch the cash just as much as they longed to explore her client's divine body. She sat on the bed and pulled out the neat wads of notes before peeling them apart one by one and dealing them out in a patchwork on the bed. Then she pulled her long hair from its clip, lay back in the sea of cash and spiked one pencil-thin heel through a crisp fifty. 'It seems to all be there,' she said, not having counted a single note. 'Which means that I'm all yours.' Adele dragged her arms through the money and rolled onto her front, giggling as she heard a champagne cork pop just like she thought she might if the mystery buyer didn't get deep inside her soon.

'Here,' he said, trailing the cold glass along the back of Adele's long legs. 'Have some of this while we talk.' He sat on the bed, his weight making Adele roll towards his thighs. She liked that.

'Talk?' She sat up and took the champagne.

'I've bought you so you have to do as I say, remember?' David rolled up the sleeves of his shirt. Adele liked the colour of his skin, the dark hairs, the length of his fingers. 'Now, tell me why you are doing this. An intelligent, beautiful young woman selling herself on the internet.'

Adele pulled a face, wondering if it was the Versace or her perfume that he didn't like. 'For the money, of course.' She took a long sip of champagne. 'And for the thrill too. Nothing excites me more than exchanging cash and if sex with a –' she drew in breath and glanced up and down his body, '– if sex with a striking man is involved too then . . .'

'You're broke, aren't you?' David poured more champagne and it seemed that he meant for a dose to spill on Adele's leg. 'I do apologise,' he said and bent down to lick it off before it dribbled onto the cash.

'How did you guess?' Her voice was barely there, shattered by his warm tongue against her skin.

'Just a hunch.' David peeled the fine fabric of Adele's dress from her legs, exposing her smooth skin right up to the edge of her tiny knickers. Then he tipped the flute just enough to spill a taste of chilled champagne onto the triangle of silk. 'At least you can afford some new ones now,' he offered before cleaning up the mess. 'Or are you so deep in debt that I'm going to have to buy you over and over again?' David eased the fabric aside and kissed her freshly marinated sex like he was kissing her mouth.

'Oh, I'm very, very deep in debt,' Adele whimpered, lying back again. One moment his tongue was buried inside her then the next it was barely there.

'And why would that be exactly?' David had already pulled off her panties and was now working on the complicated wrap-style dress but opted for ripping the fabric when he couldn't find an easy way to the rest of Adele's body.

'No!' she wailed. 'Do you know how much this dress cost?' She fingered the shredded bodice but soon gave up protesting as David unhooked her bra and doused her breasts in the remainder of his champagne.

'One thousand eight hundred and fifty pounds.'

Then he removed his shirt, spread his body over her wet breasts and kissed the indignant retort from her lips.

That he knew the exact price, Adele thought, would normally be quite remarkable but as long as his broad chest was pressed against her body and she could feel the thick hard line of his erection gathering rhythm against her thigh then she didn't care about money or debt or shopping or anything other than climaxing with the weight of this man on top of her.

'I like a woman with expensive taste.' The array of fifty pound notes beneath them crackled as David grinned and worked his way out of the remainder of his clothing. 'Let me guess,' he teased. 'Eighty to ninety thousand pounds in the red although mentally you're well on your way to the half-million mark with everything you'd like to own?'

The man's skills of deduction would have impressed Adele immensely if she hadn't been greeted by his naked erection offered conveniently to her lips. She simply nodded and sucked gratefully on the most handsome thing she had ever seen.

'I bet your bank manager loves you, with all the juicy interest you're paying.' Even through the long strokes gliding up and down his shaft, the man maintained his self-control and stayed focused on discovering just how deep Adele's financial troubles ran. He pulled out of her mouth so she could speak.

'Don't talk to me about my bank manager. Not if you want to have sex with me, anyway.' The thought of Mr Wetherby briefly curdled the thrill building between her legs.

'Oh?'

Adele thought for a moment. 'Just think the complete opposite of you. He's a miserable old man who probably hasn't had a fuck in years and he gets his kicks from hassling hard-working people like me.' She licked the silver bead forming on the end of David's cock. She really didn't want to be reminded of her bank manager at a time like this.

'I guess he's just doing his job. You know, protecting the world from shopaholics like yourself.' David gripped his purchase by the shoulders and turned her roughly onto her front. In a moment, his strong hands had lifted her hips and teased open the clear-cut line of her smooth sex. 'Have you ever actually met him?'

Adele's face melted into the cash as she felt the tip of David's erection touch her sex for the first time. 'No,' she managed, crunching a fistful of notes as he ever so slowly worked himself inside her. She moaned, really not wanting to discuss the man further.

'You're not entirely qualified to pass judgement then, are you?' Self-control slipped away with every inch that was lost inside Adele. David reached round her slim waist and ground himself so deep that it was hard to tell where his body ended and hers began.

'Guess not,' Adele capitulated breathlessly as her temporary owner moved skilfully behind her.

'Then don't you think it would be wise to wait until you see him for yourself?'

David was pounding now, sparing no thought for her reply. Her sex pulsed, gripping him, squeezing him as the first stirrings of climax spiralled within. She wanted to come a thousand times and at that moment didn't care a jot about her stupid bank manager. She had a client to please and, aside from her own delight, that was her primary consideration.

'Well?' David insisted, slowing his rhythm, leaving Adele hovering on the brink of her first orgasm. 'Don't you?' The man seemed obsessed.

'Yes, yes, OK. You're right. I should wait until I meet Mr Wetherby before I call him an uptight, nagging old git.'

David seemed to approve and cast Adele onto her back in one deft move. A shower of money rained onto the floor as he plunged inside her again, rapidly working her back to the edge of orgasm, his own climax also imminent.

Adele stared up at the man above her, hardly able to believe that her first buyer should be so perfect. She prayed that he had endless cash so that he would visit her website time and time again. Keen to ensure he did, she pulled him down by his lean, muscle-bound shoulders and wrapped her long legs around his back with her heels digging into his buttocks. She kissed him hard and afterwards he buried his lips in her long hair, working his way to her ear.

'I'm ... not ... uptight ... or miserable,' he said and then his back arced in a series of whole body spasms as the new, deep position finally tipped him over the edge.

Adele felt the hot spurts inside her as her own perfectly timed climax milked David with wave after wave of delicious orgasm. God, she should be paying *him* for the pleasure. They lay, their bodies skimmed with sweat, while Adele stroked and kissed every inch of his body. Then she stopped.

'Why say that?' she asked, sitting up and leaning over him. 'Why would I think you're in the least bit uptight or miserable?' Adele felt her cheeks colour. She didn't think she wanted him to answer.

Instead, David reached for his jeans, took out his wallet and extracted a business card. 'Always a pleasure to meet clients,' he added after handing it to Adele.

'Oh hell,' she said as she read. 'David J. Wetherby. General Manager'. Printed underneath his name and title was her bank's name and address. 'I'm even further in debt now, aren't I?' Thinking quickly, Adele plunged her mouth onto his semi-hard cock, working him back again before he could be angry.

'Deeply, deeply in debt,' he managed between involuntary gasps. 'And it's going to take an absolute age for you to pay back.'

Nick answered his telephone groggily. 'Yeah?'

'It was you, wasn't it?' Adele whispered. David was in the bathroom. Only four hours remained of the date and they'd not yet left the hotel room.

'Me what?'

'That told Mr Wetherby about my website. Go on, admit it.'

'You know Dave Wetherby?' Nick was suddenly alert.

'Well, I do now,' Adele whispered. 'Rather well, in fact. What were you doing showing him my website? He's my bank manager!'

But Adele hardly heard Nick explaining how her shopping website had accidentally become part of the presentation intended for his banking client − the same bank that Adele happened to use − because the not at all uptight or miserable Mr Wetherby had returned from the bathroom and was threatening a refund if she didn't instantly oblige his needs.

Adele smiled and snapped her phone shut while pulling him back onto the bed. 'Customer satisfaction is my main concern,' she said and got right back to work pleasing her client.

Maya Hess has written numerous short stories for Wicked Words and is the author of the Black Lace novels, *The Angels' Share* and *Bright Fire* (published 2007).